PINE BOX FOR A PIN-UP

PINE BOX FOR A PIN-UP

BY
FRANK DE BLASE

Down and Out Books, LLC
3959 Van Dyke Rd, Ste. 265
Lutz, FL 33558
www.DownAndOutBooks.com

Cover art and design by Jason Smith

ISBN: 1937495507

ISBN-13: 978-1-937495-50-3

For Deborah.

You make my jingle jangle,
my sloe-gin fizz,
my soda pop and
my sizzle sizz.

Prelude

The buxom brunette shed her top and flung it at me playfully. It didn't stop there.

"Let me get more comfortable," she said, wriggling out of the bottom half of her little leopard-print number. It was just as well; trying to contain her ample pulchritude was a losing battle. So was trying to keep my cool. She busted me mid-stare and winked. I fumbled with my camera and almost dropped it. She let out a little laugh. She'd no doubt seen men come unglued before. I was no different despite my name; it's Valentine, Frankie Valentine. I take pictures of beautiful girls.

You'd think after all the undressed pretty things I'd photographed over the years I'd be able to keep a cool head. But Vickie Hayes was something else and a half, a solid sender, a primo bombshell with a body that defied gravity. Her hair was shiny and jet black; her smile shone pearly white as it competed for attention with her dimples. At barely five feet tall, she was an abbreviated little firecracker, firmly packed and stacked into a 36-24-36 package.

I tried my best to un-blush and collect myself. I popped in a fresh roll of film and got back to it. Vickie vamped, posed and flirted with the camera as I fired away. I bounced one hot light off an umbrella to counter the mysterious shadows of the diffused key light positioned directly at her side. It gave her an eerie luster and seductive appeal. With every click of the shutter she effortlessly assumed a new pose. She needed no direction. I didn't have to say a thing, she read my mind. If I could just manage to keep it together and hold down the technical end, these were going to be some amazing photographs; hell, they were practically taking themselves. You just couldn't go wrong with a model like this. I was already planning our next session—and perhaps my next move. It was worth a shot; she seemed to like me. I couldn't wait to see her again.

But this was the last time I'd ever see Vickie Hayes...alive.

Chapter 1

The man at the bottom of the gorge had taken a shortcut, simply spread his wings and jumped, landing face up in the brush along the east side of the Genesee River.

I opted for the safer—albeit slower—route, getting snagged in the briars and wrecking my shoes while making my way down the muddy slope with a bag full of camera equipment.

I set my gear down and pulled out my handkerchief to wipe my face. I was soaked. It was summer's last hurrah. The late September sun had wasted no time warming up as it rose this morning, full blast and angry. The haze toned the brightness down some, but only added to the sizzle and stifle. The mercury was already pushing ninety degrees. We didn't get much summer here in Rochester, but when we did, we sweltered.

I trudged through the waist-high weeds, squinting to get a closer look. It was a fairly clean scene. The sudden stop at the end of his short flight had killed him instantly, but the opportune landing in the bushes helped keep his insides inside. A fall like this could often leave evidence splashed over multiple square yards. His blue suit still looked fresh and crisp despite the pulverized body inside. He hadn't been down here long, even the flies hadn't received the news yet.

Two detectives I didn't recognize were smoking and excitedly discussing last night's fight on TV with the guys from the Medical Examiner's office; Carmen

Basilio had beaten the champ, Sugar Ray Robinson, in a brutal exchange for the middleweight title.

"That Basilio's tough," one said.

"Tough?" the other said. "He's insane."

Basilio was an onion farmer turned fighter from Canastota, a little town just outside Syracuse. Local fight fans here claimed him as theirs, too. Basilio was a ruthless, relentless boxer who some say liked to get hit as much as he liked pummeling his opponents. There was no love between the two pugilists; there had been a series of heated exchanges and threats leading up to their bout at Yankee Stadium. It was one helluva fight, with our Basilio winning by decision after fifteen rounds.

I cleared my throat. They looked up.

"You tune in to the fight last night?" the one closest to me said as I approached. He let out a whoop.

"Well, I was with my own kind of knock-out last night," I said with a wink. "I was romantically detained. You know how it is." We all laughed the way guys do when alluding to a conquest that may or may not have happened. I had shot two models for a leg and stocking magazine last night. Watching those two long-legged lovelies work for the camera in little more than thigh high stockings and heels was better than watching two sweaty gorillas pound the hell out of each other. "Yeah, but I heard our boy still cleaned his clock. And speaking of which, I'm on the clock."

I opted for my Leica M3—got the camera out, mounted the .28 mm lens and flash and went to work.

This is my gig, crime scene photography. I'm a camera man, a mug snapper, a shutter bug; it's one of the safer occupations in the Rochester Police Department. By the time I make the scene, it's already over. But I get to see it all.

Suicides, murders, accidents, you name it. If there's a stiff, I'm there with my camera.

When a jilted Romeo offs his lover and himself, I'm there to document Cupid's carnage.

If the wife and the kids and the job and the bills get to be too much and Dad decides to idle the station wagon in the garage, I get to take the portrait.

The brakes fail on a steep hill; I'm at the bottom.

A tough guy brings a knife to a gun fight; me and my camera aren't far behind.

The rubbernecks were never far behind either.

Up above, a crowd had begun to gather around the railing with morbid murmurs of disappointment; aww shucks, they had just missed it.

No note, no witnesses, no indication as to what prompted his leap from the Platt Street Bridge. It's a long drop from the bridge to the sweet hereafter at the bottom, lots of time to change your mind. Yet, there wasn't a trace of fear or regret on his face. This one looked relatively peaceful, as if he were sleeping.

Empathy is fleeting when this is your line of work, and most cops harden up to keep their lunch and their sanity. Me, I wasn't so tough. I still found myself imagining the victims' last moments, the fear and dread when they absolutely knew this was it. It always gave me a chill.

I popped the close-ups of and around the victim and wider shots of the general area the detectives wanted. Using a mounted strobe helped combat the harsh morning shadows.

One of the detectives bent down and gingerly reached into the stiff's inside breast pocket. He pulled out a wallet and opened it. He pushed his hat back and groaned.

"Aww, Christ," he said. "Just when I thought we could wrap this one up easy." He reached up and handed the wallet to his partner. I leaned in to get a look.

On one side of the open billfold was a rumpled picture of two little girls in matching red dresses as they fidgeted on Santa's lap. The other side was his ID. The dead man's name was Michael Francis Conway; it was printed in bold on his private investigator's license. The late Mike Conway was a private dick. And guys in this line of work seemed to be more susceptible to "accidents" and "suicides" and general cases of misadventure than the average Joe. The fact that he was a private dick added greatly to theories other than suicide.

PI's often occupied the grey area between citizen and crook, the twilight between good and evil, where the lawless and those above the law did their dance. They had their own code. They had their own skewed sense of right and wrong. Lines got blurred, lines got crossed.

So now, in the case of Michael Conway, the probability of foul play just went up. The detectives were going to have to take that into consideration. It was going to be a long day.

I left them mulling over this development as I climbed back up to get a few shots on the bridge from the point where they determined he had jumped...or been pushed. Two beat cops were keeping the lookey-loos at bay.

The younger of the two was face to face with several bystanders who seemed reluctant to keep out of the cordoned off area. His face was beat red and didn't look old enough to shave. He was obviously new to the game; that beat cop mixture of laissez-faire diplomacy and complacency hadn't set in like it had with his more seasoned partner. He shook his head at the hot-headed rookie's zeal. He was swinging his leg as if kicking an imaginary beer can as he strolled over to me. None of what was going on seemed to affect him at all.

"Yup, yup, yup," he said, tipping his hat back to scratch his head. "What makes a fella pull a Dutch act like that?" he said. "He must've had quite a running start. If he had landed in the water, the current would've dragged him out into the lake. Then they'd be looking for him in Canada."

"He must not have wanted to get his nice suit wet," I said. We both laughed. I climbed up and leaned over the railing and my stomach immediately felt the butterfly thrill heights bring on and the nausea their consequence promised. I stopped laughing and looked down at the body.

Poor bastard, I thought.

But whatever his worries, they were all over now as they bagged and tagged and carted him away.

Chapter 2

Her silk robe fell to the floor along with my jaw. She read my reaction and giggled, motioning me to get in the tub where two more sat smiling up at me. I climbed into the warm lavender bath and sunk in.

They all spoke in Chinese and yet, for some reason, I could understand...and speak it, too. I said something back. More giggles.

Singapore.

Shore leave.

Bath time.

One sat behind with her legs wrapped around me while the other sat in my lap admiring my tattoos. The third sat on the edge of the tub washing my back. She leaned down to kiss me...

The phone's loud, ugly ring blasted me out of the tub. I almost fell out of bed, grabbing it before it had a chance to ring a second time. The voice on the other end was speaking English. The clock said 5:30 a.m. I was alone, except for Alice, the dispatcher on the other end of the horn.

"Looks like we got one for you, Frankie," she said in her trademark Upstate nasally bleat. "White female...DOA...early twenties...strangled."

I fumbled for a pen as my Chinese concubines began to fade further and further away. I grunted as I propped myself up on one elbow.

"What, did I interrupt something, lover boy?" she asked with a caffeinated laugh that graduated into a loud, raspy cough. You could practically smell the cigarettes through the phone line. "You got company?"

"I would if you weren't working," I said.

"Oh, you think so, do you?"

It went like this every time we talked; this flirty back and forth. I had never actually seen Alice, but she sounded sexy on the phone.

"So, what's the skinny?" I asked.

She rattled off the address and I started to scribble it on the back of a take-out menu.

I was halfway through jotting it down when I dropped the pen. My blood ran cold. Alice was still talking as the phone slid out of my hand.

"Frankie?" she said. "Frankie...?"

I knew this address. I picked up the receiver just to be sure.

"I-I'm on my way," I said. Alice was still talking as I hung up.

I stumbled to the bathroom half naked, half awake and completely stunned. The Mandarin narrative of my interrupted dream had made more sense. I stuck my head in the sink and stayed under, waiting for the disbelief to scatter with the fog. In my haste I got the tubes reversed and almost brushed my teeth with Brill Cream. I got dressed with whatever clothes were on the floor, grabbed my camera bag and was out the door into the waning dark of the hour.

For Joe Citizen this was the time for good morning kisses with the missus, hot coffee and a fresh squeezed start in the land of milkmen and paperboys.

However, for some, early a.m. was really just late, late p.m. And right now, for me, it was both. There was no time for coffee and my kiss was left uncollected in the distant clouds of a dirty dream.

Chapter 3

I jumped in the jalopy and crossed my fingers she'd turn over. After a little coaxing on the accelerator and pounding my fists on the dashboard, the motor fired up with a mighty Detroit roar. She was one sinister sled, although not completely reliable—a '49 Mercury two-door work in progress with a Chevy small block under the hood. It wasn't painted and sported three different colors of primer instead. I had been wrenching on it for years and was nowhere near finished. Frankly, I don't think I wanted to be done with it. Hours under the hood were a form of therapy, even though I didn't really know what I was doing. Besides, finances and time being as they were, shortcuts were taken here and there. It had no exhaust and blew right out of the manifold. The dream of twice pipes was a few paychecks away. This baby was loud. My built-in alibi; the neighbors always knew when I was coming and going, even when I didn't.

I hightailed it to the address on Arnett Boulevard Alice had given me. I knew the way. I had been there just hours before—before it was a crime scene—taking pictures of Vickie Hayes, a white female in her early twenties.

It hadn't been a date, but rather a photo shoot that went into overtime. I had played my cards right and got to spend half the night with an amazing beauty. I had been a willing victim of her charms and now she was a murder victim? No way.

You see, between all the busted valentines and chalk

outlines, the twisted wrecks and the broken necks, I spent my time photographing beautiful women, from nudie cuties to bathing beauties.

I'm not sure where the affinity came from exactly. Studying the nude female body was truly an art form handed down through the ages and I regarded it as such. However, calling myself an artist always seemed a stretch and perhaps a little high tone. I wasn't arrogant; I just wanted to be surrounded by beautiful, naked women...all the time. I've always said you make your own fun.

Vickie Hayes was one of my recent discoveries. She was beautiful. And I liked her.

I simply couldn't believe this. And now I didn't believe in red lights, stop signs or speed limits either.

The morning rush hour was in its infancy and I made it in less than five minutes; that'll happen when you don't leave any space between the gas pedal and the floor.

An orange haze had begun to form on the horizon with a warning. It was going to be another hot one. My shirt was already clinging to my back.

I rolled up on the chaos. The fanfare was lit up like a prison break by the floodlights of several squad cars jammed in the little driveway. I pulled up on the lawn and cut the motor. It backfired Howitzer-style, startling two uniformed cops standing outside. One instinctively reached for his gun.

I jumped out and sprinted past them toward the duplex, the car door left open behind me.

This was all just a big mistake, I told myself, a prank, a case of mistaken...anything. Vickie couldn't be...dead.

I pushed my way through the gauntlet of gawk clogging the front hallway. That's as far as I got.

Detective Lloyd Donovan was blocking the entire doorway from the tiny kitchen to the even tinier living room. Just past him I could see a bare foot peeking out from under the sheet. Its candy red toenail polish twinkled in contrast to the gray death in the room. That's all I could see; Donovan's seersucker bulk eclipsed the rest.

Donovan was a fat slob from the old school; blackjacks and kickbacks.

I overheard the particulars from the two uniforms first on the scene as they gave a blow-by-blow to the rest of the hat squad. Donovan was with the roommate.

She had come home late from a date to find the victim, screamed bloody murder and ran to the neighbor's to make the call. Now, she had to deal with Donovan's charm.

He was drinking from a milk carton he had helped himself to from the ice box. He wiped his mouth with his sleeve before spinning one of the kitchen chairs around backwards to sit. The roommate sat at the kitchen table stunned, shaking, crying, trying to hug herself still while she gave her statement.

She was still in a pretty cocktail dress that displayed a fine frame trembling with sobs. She tried to compose herself, dabbing at last night's makeup with a balled up tissue as it ran down her cheeks in black tears. Donovan was no help as he addressed his questions to her cleavage while continually putting his hand on her knee.

She was clearly confused and upset. Donovan's lecherous admiration, along with his unfiltered barrage of questions, didn't help. What time did she eat? Who was her date? What did he do? When was she expected home? How much had she had to drink? He didn't let up.

She answered "I don't know" to most of his questions.

"Well," he said, "I do know a girl is dead in the other room. What the hell do you know, sweetheart?" She burst into tears and ran from the room.

"I can't help 'em, if they don't cooperate," he said with a tone of exaggerated exasperation. "I'm not a mind-reader...dumb broad."

He had no respect, no decorum, no class. Not many in the room liked him. I didn't like him.

And he didn't like me, either.

We had hit it off wrong from the start after unsubstantiated rumors began circulating a few years back about Donovan's ex-wife and yours truly. When he confronted me, his tone rubbed me the wrong way—as if I couldn't land a slick chick like his ex. I was a bit naïve, new to the department and a smart aleck. And here was some fat bastard who hadn't seen his dick since VJ Day trying to high-hat me? In hindsight I should have let it drop, but I just had to say something.

"Not to worry," I assured him between loud chomps on my Juicy Fruit. "I'm sure she still loves you..."

He looked puzzled for a moment.

"Because she kept screamin' your name, Donovan," I said. I couldn't help it, I cracked myself up. There would've been a slugfest right then and there, but several guys in the squad room stepped in to wrestle us apart while wrestling unsuccessfully with the smirks on their mugs. Not everybody was wild about Donovan. A few of the old school guard were. The mysterious scratches on my car, the odd flat tire and dirty looks from his crusty cronies followed. I steered clear of him whenever I could. Sometimes, like this morning, it was unavoidable. Working with him was always a real treat.

"Wait'll you get a load of the headlights on this one, kid," Donovan said, motioning toward the body under the sheet. He wasn't really talking to me, but using me to show off. I really didn't like him.

I decided then to keep mum on my relationship with the deceased and the fact that I'd been there hours before. I wanted to see how this all played out. Besides, I didn't need to give Donovan any more ammo.

"She's dead, you slob," I said. "And I ain't your straight man, either."

"Don't you wanna take a peek, camera boy? C'mon, she's still warm."

I pushed past him and into the living room. The bickering kept me distracted and kept me cool. It would be best to appear unaffected by the scene, so I kept it up.

"I think that milk's sour," I said, pointing at my nose. "Or is it just your breath? What'd you have for breakfast? Dog shit and eggs?" He really did smell of stale cigarettes and Old Spice, really Old Spice.

He took a step towards me.

"Watch yourself, punk," he hissed. He glared down at me as I stuck a fresh piece of gum in my mouth. I balled up the foil wrapper and dropped it at his feet. I held the pack up to his face.

"Gum?" I said.

The pad was an oasis, pure Hollywood tiki lounge. And the decorator had been a dreamer wishing for nicer weather, a better locale and a better life.

In this part of Upstate New York, it snows six months out of the year due in part to its proximity to Lake Ontario. The other six go head-to-head with Seattle for the amount of days spent under an umbrella or overcast skies. Yet, this little room was straight out of the South Pacific. You could practically hear the slack-tune guitars and the crashing waves.

Hawaiian artifacts and paintings of coconut trees silhouetted by warm sunsets hung on the walls. A matching pair of rattan chairs rubbed shoulders next to a bamboo couch upholstered in dark barkcloth printed with bright tropical flowers. A little cocktail bar sat beneath the shade of a faux palm tree, while a large plaster Easter Island head cracked a grim grin. I didn't make eye contact for fear it would remember me from last night.

The place was cluttered but there wasn't much sign of a scuffle. Everything was how it had been when I left a few hours before.

Even the Martin Denny *Exotica* record she'd spun over and over was still on the little portable record player. Despite the body in the middle of the living room floor, the whole pad seemed oddly optimistic and cheery.

I surveyed the scene as if for the first time, keeping my eyes peeled for anything I might have inadvertently left behind. I had brought flowers which now sat at the base of the wall behind the couch amongst the shattered pieces of the vase Vickie had placed them in. Someone had tossed them hard. This was really the only sign tempers had flared, leading to a struggle. Donovan noticed the mess and used it as an opportunity to exert some authority and crack wise.

"Get a picture of this," he said to me as he motioned behind the couch. "Maybe whoever brought the flowers got a little sore when she wouldn't put out," he said. "I dunno, she looks like a party girl."

Donovan's partner, Angelo Rossi, was standing next to the body, drinking a cup of coffee. As opposed to Donovan, I got along with him just fine. His face was grave, but he still mustered a smile when he saw me.

"Hiya, kid," he said.

"Hey, Ange," I said. I tried not to look upset, but Rossi picked up on it straight away.

"What's the matter?" he asked with genuine concern. "You don't look so good."

"Late night, bad food, heartburn, hangover," I said, staring straight down at the true source of my malaise laying dead under the sheet.

He reached down and hoisted his trousers from above the knee as he crouched down to pull the sheet back. Rossi was a seasoned detective, ten years Donovan's senior. There was more salt than pepper in his perfectly combed hair and he always dressed sharp. He wore a dark green summer weight suit, with a red tie held by a silver tie clip. His chocolate brown wing tips were freshly shined. The man was put together. Rossi's threads weren't the latest, but rather timelessly classic. As far as I was concerned, gentlemen were always going to dress this way. Someday I would, too.

He was less than one year away from retirement—a gold watch, a slap on the back and the promise of lazy afternoons spent with a fishing pole and his two grandsons.

Rossi had been around, he'd seen everything. Still, when he uncovered the body, he bowed his head down, shaking it slowly as if maybe, just maybe, he was expecting to find something other than a dead girl under there.

"Goddammit," was all he said.

She was nude with her arms stretched over her head. One leg was crossed over the other as if she were running in place. Her head was cradled in a raven nest of hair. She stared vacant and wide-eyed at the ceiling as if she was about to say something then suddenly forgot. I crouched down to look. Her skin was cold and blue-ish. I felt mine turning green-ish and damp; I couldn't breathe. I stood up too quickly and almost blacked out. Yup, it was Vickie Hayes. She had been strangled. And my tie was wrapped tightly around her neck.

Chapter 4

Vickie Hayes was a knockout beauty with plenty of poise and moxie. Most models around here were more earthy and into figure study-type work as they posed for khaki-wearing bohemian eggheads with charcoal pencils. The area's brief summers probably didn't help either. Swimsuit season here barely lasted two months and the bathing beauty was a rare bird. Vickie was an extraordinary bird—my kind of ornithology.

We had met through mutual friends while catching Bull Moose Jackson one night a couple of years ago at The Cotton Club over on Joseph Avenue.

This show was a big deal for Rochester fans who dug their music on the savage side. Jackson recorded for King Records. The old jukebox at Patsy's, my favorite bar that didn't have live music, was filled with King Records' platters or "lacquer crackers" as Jackson called them. It was the stuff that positively sent me.

I dug jazz and routinely hit hot spots around town like The Band Box or The Ridge Crest Inn, but The Cotton Club booked the stuff I really liked; rough, raw, sexy, bluesy sounds the other joints didn't want to take a chance with on account of the rowdy audience it drew and drove wild. Jackson was one of those musicians. He sang in a wailing baritone and swung on the sax as if it were a rusty axe. And tunes like *I Want a Bowlegged Woman*, *Nosey Joe* and *Big Ten Inch Record* were double—in some cases single—entendre tunes that were certified crowd pleasers and fuse-lighters.

Jackson and his pick-up band made up of local cats

had barely gotten through his opening number and already had the crowd boiling when I first laid eyes on Vickie Hayes as she tried to sit alone at the bar. She had charm and she had guts as she fended off come-on after come-on. She moved to the dance floor, but the wolves followed and their pitches intensified. She was the only white woman in the place.

But it wasn't the men in the joint that posed a threat. It was their women who didn't appreciate being upstaged by some white girl their men made no attempt to ignore. They eased up on the dagger eyes and the whispering once I came to the rescue and she and I started our own party at our own table. I remember thinking, *This is The Cotton Club, not the land of cotton.* Sadly, Rochester wasn't nearly as progressive as it thought.

I had hoped the music would have contributed to an evening-long cease-fire of dancing and knocking one or two back. But good ol' rhythm'n'blues-stained rock'n'roll, like the kind Jackson was blasting off the bandstand, tended to get folks out of their seats and on their feet. It also got them good and fired up sexually, physically and left with one of two options: ramp up the romance with the one you were with—or the one you were going to be with—or start a fight. I've experienced both urges and they aren't all that different.

We met several times for a drink and I'd see her at shows now and then, but it would be a couple years before our first and only shoot. She didn't offer a lot of personal info, but I gathered just by the way she had danced alone that night at The Cotton Club, she liked a good time and was unattached–unattached, but not necessarily unattainable.

This was my reasoning behind showing up with flowers last night and perhaps the reasoning behind the aftershave, too. But I was no Romeo-on-the-spot; it seemed a little early to shift from pro to beau. There were already enough meatheads, morons and panty-sniffers with cameras just out for cheap thrills and I didn't want to get lumped in with them. So when we shot last night, it was strictly on the up and up. If we stayed nothing more than friends, well, that was fine with me. I would just follow her lead. And yes, I believe I meant that. I had convinced myself anyway.

I kept it light even when she spilled about her current man trouble. I was more than willing to listen and nod and frown disapproval over this cad's lack of couth. I was a sensitive guy after all and *Yes*, I agreed, *all men were pigs*, even though I was vying to be the next swine in line.

The source of her grief was married and twice her age. She strung him along for a little cash and a good time, but had inadvertently fallen for his play.

Vickie had rolled plenty of these silver-haired Romeos before and was more than willing to live beyond their means. But for a change, there wasn't the romantic letdown that often came with seniority. Usually these love affairs were more about fiscal—than physical—fitness, however according to Vickie, he was quite the talent: a real mattress dancer. He had lit her fuse and it wasn't going out. She wanted more.

But he held "a position of prominence and couldn't afford a scandal." So where she had been promised romantic getaways and a taste of the good life, it all came down to sweaty afternoon romps at hot pillow joints like the Cavalier Motel on Mt. Hope where love gets paid for by the hour. She had had enough of not getting enough. Now, he had stopped returning her phone calls. This was unwise.

"What are you gonna do?" I asked.

"Oh, he's a special one," she said. "He likes his picture taken, too." She laughed when she said it but her eyes flashed hot. "He's not nearly as photogenic as I am, though. I'm gonna get him where it hurts." And I knew damn well she could. Folks who documented their lust lives usually lived to regret it. Pictures like this always had a way of surfacing at the wrong time.

There really were only two ways to put the hurt on one of these aging playboys: the family jewels or the family fortune. Whichever route Vickie chose to take, he was certainly gonna feel it.

"Just be careful, honey," I said, knowing in reality she wasn't the one in danger. She snapped back in a smoky purr.

"You be careful," she said. "And keep your mouth shut."

I held my hands up.

"I don't know nothin' from nothin'," I said, picking my camera back up.

The burning anger in her eyes quickly cooled to a slow smolder as she posed in a two-piece leopard print number on her bamboo bar. It was at least one size too small. It was times like these I congratulated myself on my career choice. Vickie wasn't just beautiful. She moved beautifully as well—languid, smooth, sublime.

She laughed a lot and seemed comfortable, even when her outfit hit the floor.

After we wrapped it up and I had packed up my lights and gear, we sat on the lounge sipping beers and listening to records. She sat close to me, one leg tucked beneath her. She never bothered to get dressed and I never bothered to suggest she do so. I was numb with desire. She was nude except for my necktie, which she had playfully tied around her neck. It was starting to get warm when she got up to flip the record over for the third time. I rolled the dice and pulled her onto my lap. She didn't resist. I had rolled a seven and went to heaven.

"I was wondering when you were going to make a move," she said, wallowing into me.

"I wasn't sure you dug me like that," I said.

"Oh, on the contrary. You give me a large charge, daddy-o."

She kissed me hard. I kissed back. For the next hour it was all a torrid tornado of legs and arms and those soft accessories that make a man crazy.

I guess the flowers worked.

Chapter 5

Even now in death with the incomplete expression on her cold face, Vickie's beauty was undeniable. My heart ached.

I mouthed her name under my breath, but the sound came out from somewhere behind me.

"Vickie Hayes," somebody whispered. "Holy shit, isn't she Eddie Hayes' kid?"

I spun around and looked up to Rossi. He put his finger to his lips before motioning me aside. He looked grave. He gave me the skinny on Eddie Hayes.

Eddie Hayes was a hard-boiled ex-cop, praised and admired by all, a cop who went by his own book. He cracked cases, he cracked heads, he almost cracked up. Cops would get all doe-eyed like star-struck bobby-soxers when telling tales of this urban legend. He got bigger each time. At this rate, he was going to be over ten feet tall by 1960. Even Rossi had a crush on him.

Eddie Hayes was a legend before my time. Tough as nails...spent time in a POW camp in the Philippines during the war. He was aces at hostage negotiation and left very few cases open when he left. But when the daily grind began to grind him down, he swapped out his shield for a PI ticket and did mostly private security work, background checks and such.

Hayes' swan song, so the story goes, was a bank robbery gone sideways on Genesee Street. The perp—later linked to a string of heists throughout the Upstate area—was almost all the way through with a sizable withdrawal from Federal Savings and Loan when a young teller hit the alarm. He panicked and shot her dead, along with the security guard who had tried to intervene. The hapless crook tried to barter with the lives of the eight remaining employees and four customers. Hayes spent all of ten minutes on the bullhorn with him before he marched in and coolly shot him twice in the head—real cowboy stuff. The crook never got off a shot. Hayes was a hero, but the brass thought he might be getting just a tad too fast and loose. He went into private practice after that. It was a mutually agreed upon "retirement."

And now, his daughter lay dead before me where just hours before she had been vibrant and alive in my arms. Nobody needed to know that. Especially, Eddie Hayes. Keeping my mouth shut made even more sense now.

"He's still a pretty high-strung cat," Rossi said. "We have to handle this carefully. He's gonna go crazy."

I slipped in a roll of Kodachrome and popped off my camera's lens cap. I mounted the flash and the same wide-angle lens I'd used last night and went through the motions of getting to work. I felt sick. I was sweating and shaking, fumbling with my gear. I didn't want to let on that I knew her, at least until I knew what was going on. Donovan didn't need any help or excuse if presented with the opportunity to complicate my life.

Had her blackmail scheme gone sour? Who was the man in the pictures she'd told me about? Did he kill her? Where were these pictures now? Why the hell did I forget my tie?

I moved around the room to capture the various aspects and angles of the crime scene. I could still smell her perfume. Donovan continued with the chin music.

"Smile, honey," he said.

"Put a sock in it, Lloyd," Rossi said. He deserved a medal for enduring this asshole on a daily basis.

Donovan wouldn't let up. I continued to shoot.

"This dame oughta look good in your portfolio, camera boy. She's drop-dead gorgeous." He roared and poked the uniform next to him. "Get it? Drop dead gor...."

I folded him in half with a punch to his extra-large gut. He dropped to one knee. In an instant, everyone in the room was between us, the vicarious intoxication of an impending fight in their eyes. Protocol had them split us up before any more blows were exchanged and it got bloody. But if we'd really wanted to throw down, they would have backed off. And Donovan probably would have clobbered me.

"You sonofabitch," he said, wheezing for air. "Why're you so touchy? You know this broad?"

I didn't answer.

Perhaps I should have. I began packing up my gear. I had enough shots and needed to get the hell out of there.

You could hear his hinges creak as he slowly got back to his feet. He spit on the floor and looked right at me.

"Son of a bitch. You do know this broad, don't you, smart guy?" He moved toward me. I shoved past him and began to make my way for the door. He grabbed my shoulder and spun me around.

"Hey," he shouted. "What is this stiff to you, shitbird?"

"She's somebody's daughter," I said, my voice wavering just a bit.

"Every skirt is somebody's daughter," Donovan said. "Who's this broad's daddy, then?"

Rossi pulled him aside. They spoke in hushed tones for half a minute before Donovan returned to his normal volume.

"Hayes? What do I care? He doesn't pull any weight around here anymore."

Rossi's fists instinctively balled up, his nostrils flared.

He glared at Donovan. Donovan was bigger, but Rossi was boxer-lean and in excellent shape. Donovan got the hint; he was out of line. He backed down.

"So how's the kid here involved?" he asked. "Tell me that, huh? What's he hiding?"

They both looked at me.

I didn't stick around to answer and beat feet out to my car. I fired it up and stood on the gas, kicking up grass and dirt into the air until the rubber hit the road with a loud squeal.

Chapter 6

I didn't sweat Donovan. He didn't have anything on me. There was nothing to be had other than the fact I had been at the crime scene mere hours before, other than the fact my necktie was the apparent murder weapon, other than the fact I was one of the last people to see Vickie alive. Yeah, other than that, everything was jake. I was clean.

I was screwed.

I didn't need to be implicated in a murder. Innocent or not, Fatso would have no problem hanging something—anything—on me. I shook my head hard. Maybe if I re-jumbled the few remaining marbles along with what I knew so far, it might make sense. But I didn't really know anything. I shook my head again just in case. When the rattling stopped, I didn't know anything new, just that Vickie was still dead. Somehow I had to figure out the rest.

My studio was in a loft on the fourth floor of the Cox Building on St. Paul Street. I was never at my stuffy little apartment so I gave it up and now this was my full-time crib as well. Though business and pleasure were the same thing in my case, I still liked having the option of separating the two when I wanted. So I built a giant raised area ten feet off the floor. It was my bedroom and lounge, my plateau of solitude. Below was a little efficiency kitchen and next to that, the bathroom. The rest of the pad was wide open except for assorted light stands, backdrops and props—perfect for constructing whatever scenarios I could come up with.

I took the freight elevator up four flights. It was so hot I would've drowned in my own juices on the stairs. I got to my place and jumped in the shower and stood there until I was numb from the cold water beating down on me. I had a cold shave which left enough nicks and cuts on my face so I looked like I'd slow danced cheek to cheek with a cactus. Toweling off was futile. Sweat simply replaced the water. I gave up and got dressed in a thin yellow cotton shirt and baggy black twill trousers.

Shower, shave, fresh duds—this was supposed to make a man feel better, and usually it did. But this morning there were heavy things going on in my head...potentially heavy things hanging over my head as well.

Chapter 7

I stopped by Carl's Cameras on Lyell Avenue to pick up whatever he had ready. The crime lab took care of the police stuff, but the girlie pics were brought to life here.

Almost every aspect of photography fascinated me though I never felt the need to slosh around in chemicals. I left that to Carl. I had inherited the shutterbug from my old man, who shot wildlife and nature. I did the same, so to speak.

Capturing a moment with my trusty Leica or Speed Graphic, proving I was there. Playing with shadows, catching a model's come-hither glance and temporal beauty—that's why I took pictures. It was how I experienced and truly appreciated beauty of the female form and the indiscriminate ugliness and finality of death. Yeah, the nudie cuties were intoxicating, but the crime scenes were a little sobering. It all balanced out. There was often a certain depravity—an ugly beauty—that preceded both schools which I found fascinating.

Now, both worlds were colliding.

Carl was hip to beauty. He shot glamour as well, real classic cheesecake stuff, starting with the liberated libertines and mademoiselles in post-war France, where he served with the press corps. An avid hunter, he had bagged a grizzly in British Columbia and had it resurrected as a rug. It served as a prop for a lot of his shoots. "Bares on a bear" he called them. It was an ongoing project. He had met two of his ex-wives this way. Carl was the one who turned me on to some of my biggest photographic influences, pros like Russ Meyer, Peter Gowland and Irving Klaw.

Carl got my style and his savvy in the darkroom had saved more than a few shots I had cropped weird or underexposed in my enthusiasm and haste. It's sometimes hard to focus when you're focusing on a beautiful girl.

He would tell me, "When you shoot pretty girls, you've got to keep it together. You've got to stay focused. Don't drool. You've gotta be cool, fool."

He was a friendly guy despite the military uniform he always wore, complete with a side arm. Carl was a bit of a gun nut. He never left the war entirely; it followed him home.

He was stuffing prints and a contact sheet into an envelope as I walked in. Between the static, crackle and hiss of the little transistor radio on the counter WBBF's Nick Nickson "The Ol' Professor" was carrying on about the unusual September heat wave. Carl looked up when he heard the bell on the door jingle and smiled a big smile.

"Yessir," he said, sliding the envelope across the counter towards me. "She's a beauty. If she don't turn you on, man, you've got no switches. Where'd you find this one anyway?" I opened it up and my heart sank; it was Vickie. I had popped the rolls from the shoot in Carl's overnight drop box. I mustered a smile at half-mast.

"Man, that was fast," I said.

"Well, you know Robert," he said. "He saw it was one of your orders and prepped it first thing this morning. He likes your girls a whole lot."

"That makes two of us," I said.

Robert was Carl's old lady's younger brother. Robert was a little slow and essentially unemployable. He was a giant, well over six feet tall with the smarts of a four-year-old and the libido of a teenager. Carl kept him busy around the shop, cleaning up, changing fixers and prepping rolls of film.

He knew his way around a camera and was always pestering me to take him along to a shoot. I didn't want to hurt his feelings but that was never going to happen. I had to let him down slow when he first cornered me a couple of years ago.

"The one with the long legs," he said. "Yeah, the long legs. She's pretty. I like her, I like her."

"I don't know, Bob," I said. "She's pretty shy. And besides, a good lookin' fella like you, who knows what she'd do."

"But, Frank, I just want to take her picture."

"Yeah, buddy, I use that line a lot, too."

He had a better chance at getting pictures of J. Edgar Hoover shaving his legs in a bubble bath. Robert had already been caught a coupla times peeking in neighbors' windows with his pants down. The poor guy didn't mean any harm. If it weren't for Carl, it's anyone's guess where Robert would have wound up.

My jobs scratched his voyeur itch and I knew he made copies for himself. I didn't mind; they made him happy and they kept him off the street.

Ordinarily, I'd be happy too, picking up a new set of shots, especially when they came out this good. But I was clearly distracted. Carl took notice of my mood.

"Why so glum, chum?" he asked.

Within a matter of hours I had taken Vickie's last living and first dead photos.

I gave Carl the *Reader's Digest* version. He was already privy to the whole Donovan debacle. But his eyes got big when I spilled this news.

"I was just there, Carl," I said. "Donovan's got it in for me and Hayes isn't gonna take a back seat on this, either."

Carl's eyes got bigger for a second. He stared at me.

"What?" I said. "You know something?"

"No, of course not. What do I know anyway?" he said, enunciating a little too perfectly to be telling the truth. He was lying. It was written all over his face. Obviously neither one of us played much poker.

"C'mon, Pinocchio," I said. "Give."

He hesitated, licking his lips.

"Well..." he said. "Mickey was in here two weeks ago with some, you know, pictures of, well, this same girl and, or I mean with...."

I butted in. "Lemme guess, an older gentleman?"

Carl didn't say anything, but I knew.

Mickey Miller.

Mickey Miller was a real Tijuana Bible-beater. He produced stag films, burlesque reels and blue movies like those you could see in the underbelly of major metropolitan tenderloins across the map. But for gents around here who wanted a little X-rated look-see on poker night or on the eve of their walk down the aisle, Mickey's movies like *Dolly's Double D Double Take*, *Jungle Love*, my personal favorite *The Naughty Night Nurse* and *Bonnie and the Burro* were the ticket.

Mickey was going nationwide with these sin-sational cinematic delights as the major markets throughout the U.S.—New York City, Hollywood, etcetera—had bigger vice clampdowns to deal with. Thanks to the Kefauver hearings in 1955, their police departments had whole divisions dedicated to squashing smut peddlers and keeping League of Decency blowhards quiet. In the relatively wholesome city of Rochester, Mickey and his crew flew below radar to feed the ever-growing demand for decadence around the country.

Mickey was a decent photographer but had gotten the taste for the bigger payday this vocation afforded him. He wasn't a bad cat and we were pretty good friends, but some of his associates and backers were bad news. He ran with some pretty fast characters, characters Carl didn't want to cross.

But there was more to Carl's story.

"Then yesterday," he said, "a detective, one of those gun-for-hire types, you know, a private investigator, came around here asking all kinds of questions about pornography and Mickey and a set of photos that I assumed are the ones I did for Mickey...the ones you're talking about."

"What did you tell him?"

"Bupkis. He tried the tough guy routine with me, but no soap. He left with nothing. Oh, but he left a card."

"Let me see it," I said.

Carl reached over to the cork board on the wall behind the counter, pulled off a business card and handed it to me. It read: *Conway Private Investigations, Michael Conway, Pres., Criminal-Civil-Domestic* with an address in the Powers Building downtown and a number.

"What the hell?" I said. It was the dead guy from the gorge. A concerned look was beginning to crease Carl's face.

"What the hell is going on here anyway?" he said. "I'm not in the mood for any trouble."

"How many sets did you print for Mickey?" I asked.

"Two."

"Then you've—we've—got trouble."

"What should I do?" Carl asked.

"I'll let you know as soon as I do," I said as I headed slowly for the door lost in thought.

I was beginning to connect the dots. Vickie was putting the squeeze on her co-star, what with his "position of prominence" and all, and he killed her. It was failed blackmail. Mickey was the shutter man and not entirely above pulling a short con to make a quick buck or a shady dollar here or there himself. So Mickey had Carl print up doubles. Someone had hired a PI to find these pictures and he wound up as body number two. I needed to find Mickey pronto.

Chapter 8

The door was closed and you could still hear him.

"Valentine," Captain Sam Prescott bellowed from his office. He was loud and articulate. He never had to repeat himself and nobody ever asked him to speak up. He had a built-in bullhorn. Prescott had worked his way up through the blue ranks from beat cop to the top. He was linebacker-large with an extremely flat flattop. His barber maintained it with a level. It seemed to me that he was still growing; his pants were always too short and he looked ready to bust out of his sports jacket. If he would just go up a shirt size or so, his face would probably lose a good deal of its ever-present rosiness. There was no Mrs. Prescott to dress him at home. As far as I knew, there never had been. He was married to the job.

The older guys in the department called him "Prez." I didn't have to work with him all that much, but when I did he and I got along just fine.

I hadn't been there long enough for familiarities.

"Yes, Captain?"

He was pouring over some papers on his desk.

He didn't look up.

"You have a run-in with Donovan this morning?" he asked.

I tried to play it off, giving him the rundown, the milk, the remarks, the sobbing roommate.

"He just pushed my buttons and I'd had enough," I said.

"Look," Prescott said, "I'm not his number one fan and I know he's a little crude, but he's a good cop."

"That's debatable," I said.

Prescott let out a long sigh. He looked exasperated. Donovan had probably already dimed, tattled his side and I hadn't gained any popularity by supposedly fraternizing with fatso's wife. With cops it was unwritten but understood: you don't fool around with another cop's wife—current, ex or otherwise.

"Frankie, he thinks you know something about the dead girl or that you're somehow involved."

"Yeah? Well, he also thinks gravy is a beverage."

I didn't expect any laughter. I didn't get any either. Perhaps Prescott was waiting for the rim-shot.

"Did you know the victim?"

It might have been a good time to be upfront, but instinctively I dummy'd up. I wasn't a suspect, except maybe in Donovan's eyes. Donovan, he could go piss up a rope. I copped an angelic mug and made a gesture that was part Boy Scout salute, part sign of the cross, part cross-my-heart-and-hope-to-die.

"Nope. Just felt bad for the girl, that's all," I said. "Look, talk to Rossi. He was there."

The phone on Prescott's desk jangled loudly. He winced and grabbed it in the middle of the second ring. He offered no salutation; the voice on the other end was already in full gab. Prescott grunted a few single-syllable responses before he hung up.

"We're going to need to see your photographs from the Hayes scene right away," he said. "Something doesn't add up."

"What?" I asked, a little nervous.

"You don't worry about it. Just do your job...and stay out of Donovan's hair."

The Captain dismissed me with a wave. He had picked up the receiver and was dialing a number as I left the room, closing the door slowly behind me in hopes of hearing something.

"Yeah, I've got a problem," he was saying. "I just got off the phone with the medical examiner...The Hayes girl wasn't strangled...You heard me...I'm aware of the necktie...No, it wasn't the cause of death...No, a broken neck...That's right...The tie was probably put there post-mortem to throw us off."

Or to set me up, I thought.

I was still hanging around the Captain's door as low key as I could, trying to blend into the wall and make out what I could through the wood.

So, somebody had broken Vickie's neck and gave her a post-mortem Windsor knot with my necktie. Why?

I could feel a similar noose around my neck.

It was just a matter of time before Donovan put me and Vickie together. And Eddie Hayes would be hot on the trail like Bulldog Drummond as well.

The noose was tightening. The clock was ticking.

But once I talked to Mickey, I'd get ahold of these photos—the batch Carl had already seen—and figure out just who Vickie's so-called "distinguished gentleman" was. Yup, that's what I'd do. Then I'd hand over the info to Rossi. They'd have Vickie's killer, I'd be in the clear, and I'd get the chance to burn Donovan at the detective game as a bonus.

I walked past the sign-in area where a particularly loud customer was raising all kinds of hell. He looked steamed. He pounded his fist on the counter so hard the stapler and assorted clipboards jumped as high as the poor receptionist behind the desk. He had her frazzled. She began randomly organizing papers on her desk that were already organized. She pushed her cat eye glasses back up with a trembling hand and looked up at his immense frame.

This character was a brick wall in brogans, somewhere in his late fifties. He wore a short-sleeved shirt barely containing the two burly pythons emerging from each sleeve. He had a grown-out, salt and pepper crew cut on top of a huge head, which rested on an even huger neck. He was clearly in a bad mood and looked as if he wasn't all that familiar with good ones. I slowed down to get the lowdown. The receptionist was still trying to talk him down while dealing with her own panic.

"S-sir," she said. "The Captain is very...he's v-very busy."

"Is that right?" he asked.

The girl nodded.

"Well, I don't give a good goddamn," he shouted. "I want to see Prescott! Now! You tell him Eddie Hayes is here. Eddie Hayes. He knows who I am. He'll see me."

Eddie Hayes.

I put my hand in front of my face as if I were shielding my eyes from the sun. Hayes and I didn't need to meet now, or ever for that matter. I made tracks out of there in double time.

The noose was getting even tighter.

Chapter 9

I drove around aimlessly for about an hour, collecting my thoughts and strategizing as if I knew what to do. My brain and the car were running on fumes by the time I rolled into the Sunoco. The car stalled at the pump. My brain kept going, bombarding me with all that was going on and all I didn't understand about it.

While the Merc was getting gassed up, I walked over to the pay phone. I wasn't sure if anyone would answer when I called Conway's office. Obviously Conway wouldn't, but maybe he had a partner, an assistant, a secretary, anybody who could shed some light. A young voice picked up on the first ring.

"Conway Private Investigations," she said.

I went headlong into my unrehearsed ploy.

"Mister Conway, please," I said. There was a short pause before she answered.

"I'm sorry," she said. "Mister Conway is unavailable. Perhaps you would like to leave a message with Mister Chapman. He's handling Mister Conway's cases for the time being."

"Oh, Conway's gone?" I asked. "When do you expect him back?"

"He didn't say," she said. "He makes his own hours. He is the boss, after all." She wasn't giving up a thing. "Would you like to leave a message for Mister Chapman?"

"Yeah," I said. "I would. Tell him it's about the photographs."

Chapter 10

It was early evening when I set out to look for Mickey. He wasn't hard to find. He hung out at The Bamboo Club on East Avenue. And it was easy to see why. The Bamboo Club was a tiny burlesque joint—about three times the size of a phone booth—catering to folks who liked to tie one on as the girls took it off, bump'n'grind with a twist of lime.

It was intimate, as the crowd was shoehorned in elbow-to-elbow to take in a striptease act that was practically in their laps, given the establishment's diminutive layout. The gals at The Bamboo Club all had maximum peel and squeal appeal, with torrid displays of agility and anatomy that periodically had owner Hy Isaacs in court explaining this was art and the girl in question was convent-bred and taking care of her sickly mother.

I strolled in as a large breasted and rather callipygian dancer on sparkly heels was in the final stretch of her routine. She was what some might call plump, but something I just considered busty all over—built for comfort, my kind of gal.

The strip portion was over and now it was all about the shimmy and shake. This gal was wholeheartedly shaking her backside into a delicious blur. 'Round and 'round it went just like the mesmerized eyes of the guys in front.

I walked in, parked on a vacant barstool and watched as she bent over backwards, spinning her tassels in opposite directions to the whistles, hoots and hollers from the left-over-from-happy-hour set.

As salacious as it was, I was preoccupied. I signaled the barkeep for a beer and inquired about Mickey. Initially, he didn't know him, but after several beers and some arm twisting—with a little help from the late Mister Lincoln—he agreed to pass along my message. I left The Bamboo Club as the next ecdysiast came out, already pulling one of her opera gloves off with her teeth.

"Ladies and gentlemen," the MC barked. "It is my distinct pleasure to present for your distinct pleasure... Miss Dusty Fox!"

Any other time and I would have stayed but I was a bit tipsy and too overwhelmed to appreciate it.

Chapter 11

I had parked the sled in a slot on Gibbs Street just before the Eastman Theatre and was making my way back to it when I noticed a tall character in a short-sleeve shirt and tie leaning against it. He was cleaning the ashes from his pipe by tapping it sharply against his heel.

"Mister Valentine?" the man asked as I approached. I couldn't place him.

"Maybe," I said.

"Look, pal, you called me about some photographs."

"Right," I said. "You must be Chapman."

"Yeah, I must be."

"There's a little coffee shop that's open around the corner," I said. "Let's talk there."

We took two spots at the counter and ordered up some vintage coffee from yesterday by the looks and taste of it.

"So," Chapman said, squinting through a sip of sour java, "you've got some pictures for me?"

"I have some pictures for Mike Conway, actually."

"Conway's indisposed."

"More like disposed of...permanently. Look, let's stop playing games, Chapman."

I gave him the abridged version of my bio and how I was privy to what few facts there were.

"Some pictures were taken," I said. "Perhaps on the sly, I don't know—blackmail, extortion, whatever. As a result, a friend of mine is dead. Your pal Conway was sniffing around and now he's dead, too."

"You don't know what you're dealing with here, Valentine," Chapman said.

"Neither do you," I shot back.

"Exactly. That's why this case worries me. According to Mike, these are big people with everything to lose and the means not to."

"Case?" I asked. "This is your case now?"

"My partner's dead. I have to find out who did it."

"Who was Conway working for?"

"Some judge. Never did get the name. He didn't really want to discuss it with me and it was strictly a hush-hush deal around the office. He did say that he'd gotten a lead on some pictures and that the client was loaded. How does your friend figure in?"

"Vickie had an affair with this character," I said. "And she's the one, I think, that might've set up the picture scheme."

Chapman set his coffee cup down into its saucer with a loud clink. It spilled a little. He leaned forward.

"Wait a minute. Vickie?" he asked in a loud whisper. "Vickie Hayes? Eddie Hayes' kid?"

I nodded three times.

"And he thinks I'm somehow involved," I said. Chapman started to laugh, before downing the rest of his toxic joe.

"Good luck with that, pal," he said.

Chapter 12

I had a few hours to kill until Mickey would be up or just getting home from the previous night's low jinks. I spent the better part of the afternoon getting the car washed, killing time with the magazines at Ehman's newspaper nest in the RG&E building's main lobby and nursing a lemonade at the diner counter while I started to read the newspaper front to back. Vickie's murder was below the fold and near the bottom, but front page news just the same. The story's headline stopped me cold. It was real now. Seeing it in print made it seem a little more true. Still, I had a hard time believing it.

STRANGLER SOUGHT IN HAYES' MURDER it read in bold, underscored with *Police Have Few Clues in Glamour Model/Student's Killing.* Apparently investigators were keeping mum to the fact they didn't believe she was strangled. This was a frequent strategy set in place to weed out actual suspects from attention-starved psychos who popped up to confess for a shot at notoriety.

The daily *Democrat and Chronicle* didn't usually gravitate to the salacious side of stories like these, so the details of the crime that followed were rather vanilla, vague and devoid of any real specifics or juicy tidbits. There was a high school yearbook photo of Vickie which, despite the toned-down make-up and ponytail, still showed her breathtaking beauty. It didn't mention any family other than her father—"the infamous top cop Eddie Hayes"—or mention any background. It occurred to me, despite my budding fondness, I really knew nothing about her. There were quotes from Donovan about "good leads" and "persons of interest" and an "any day now" timeline, but nothing of any substance, really. Hopefully Mickey would have more news.

Four o'clock, he'd be up by now. I was about to hang up after the tenth ring when he finally picked up. He agreed to meet me.

"I'll buy ya a cheeseburger," he said.

I was always in the mood for a Don and Bob's ground round. I'd been eating there since before my feet touched the ground, sitting next to my old man on one of the stools at the counter. I pointed the bomb north on Culver and made a beeline for Seabreeze with a roar.

Mickey was already seated at the counter working on a root beer and the counter girl when I walked in. She was first-rate whistle bait and Mickey was pouring it on heavy and sweet. She giggled, twirling her hair around her finger as her eyes darted around nervous and shy. She was all grown up on the outside, but a little too fresh off the farm on the inside to realize what power she actually possessed over men—which made her perfect for Mickey. My entrance cut the audition spiel short.

"No, really, you could be an actress," he was saying. "Look, just come down to my studio and we.... Frankie, whaddaya say?"

He stood up to greet me like he was selling a car, his hand outstretched.

"How ya doin', how ya doin'?" he asked enthusiastically, a toothpick bobbing in the corner of his mouth beneath a pencil-thin mustache. I covered my eyes in mock blindness. Mickey had a penchant for loud Hawaiian shirts and this particular number could've drowned out an air raid siren—when I closed my eyes I could still see it. His blue gabardine slacks were equally bright and he wore a cocoa-colored summer straw with a stingy brim. He made Cuban-heeled tracks in alligator roach killers. Mickey was sure enough slick, like a pimp in an Easter parade. Next to him in my T-shirt, jeans and sneakers, I looked black and white, if anyone saw me at all.

"That chick's too young to fry, don't you think?" I asked, motioning my head toward the counter girl. Mickey just laughed.

"Save your breath, pal," he said. "You're preaching to the perverted." We both laughed.

We ordered up a couple cheeseburgers and chocolate malts and adjourned to a booth by the window. I wasted no time and told him about Vickie.

"Aw, that's terrible," he said. "She was a real sweet kid."

I bypassed our usual shuck'n'jive and braced him right off.

"Look," I said, "I don't want to jam you up, but how deep are you into this?" Mickey was a pro. He had been lying and hustling for years, but I thought he went on the defensive perhaps a little too quick.

"Frankie, you've got it all wrong," he said. "This weren't no blackmail hustle, honest. Sure I've put the squeeze on hubbies on the extra-curricular stroll before, but this was strictly on the perv; Casanova here got off on being photographed, on being watched. It was like he was bragging for the camera."

Mickey continued with his mouth full.

"He was an animal," he said. "Banged her like an old screen door. It just went on and on and on until she passed out. Guy must take his vitamins. Besides, he was some kind of weirdo; he had her take a..."

I cut him off.

"The pictures."

"What?"

"What did you do with the pictures, Mick?" I asked.

He took a casual pull off his malt.

"Gave 'em to Vickie who I guess gave 'em to the old stallion once I had 'em developed."

"And the negs?"

"Ditto. What was I gonna do with them?"

I raised my eyebrows. I was still skeptical. "Really? Who was this guy?" I asked.

"I have no idea. A suave, older cat...a real charmer. I mean, we weren't formally introduced."

My eyebrows went higher. Mickey looked around cautiously. He leaned forward and spoke low.

"On the level, Frankie," he said. "Look, Rosa said this was a need-to-know gig and that I didn't need to know. All I know is I got a nice stack of greenbacks out of the deal."

"Wait," I said. "You said Rosa. Rosa Lee?"

"Yup. Rosa Lee. Say, weren't you two..."

"Yeah, we...I mean, no...I mean it's complicated."

Rosa was a retired stripper turned madam who represented an impressive stable of models for artists, print work, runway work, TV and film appearances and various gigs around the country. On the surface, it was a legit operation. However, she also provided dates for big wigs, captains of industry, well-to-do gentlemen and politicos in need of a glamorous arm charm for an event or weekend getaway. Rosa's girls were sugar babies for sugar daddies.

So, Rosa was in on this. That meant Vickie was working for Rosa as one of her call girls. It didn't bother me as much as the jealous pangs wafting up from the images Mickey's story planted in my head, "It just went on and on and on until she passed out."

Chapter 13

The sun was a bright orange ball dipping into the horizon; the remnants of its unseasonable heat still had the city in a slow bake. I left Mickey back at the hamburger joint waiting for his next starlet to finish her shift. Turns out she needed a ride.

I hung a left off East Main onto Genesee Street where a gaggle of little kids splashed in the spray from an open hydrant, laughing and squealing loudly as I rolled by. A fine mist from the blast spritzed me through the open window—it was so hot I could hear it sizzle on my skin.

It was almost dark and the old man living next door to Vickie's was busting his knuckles on a late model Ford, trying to get it started, despite the number of crucial parts still scattered about the driveway along with half a dozen empty beer cans. He wore greasy coveralls and an equally greasy cap. He was cursing loudly over a symphony of cicada bugs, but stopped when he saw me approach.

I work for the police department, but I'm not exactly a cop. In fact, I'm not a cop at all. I don't wear a badge and I don't carry a gun. So I flashed my department ID quickly and started in with the Q&A before he could object or get suspicious. When you brace them quick, they don't get time to think or to doctor up the story, so you're more likely to get the truth. Often, as in this case, it can go on and on.

Vickie's roommate "Had gone to stay with her folks in Buffalo...he had been entrusted with a key to water the plants and keep an eye on things while the roommate was away...no, nobody had been around, and wasn't it a shame...such a nice girl...you just don't know these days...his missus was afraid to leave the house..." and so on.

I made some weak excuse about leaving the "official crime scene key" at headquarters and wouldn't he be a good citizen and loan me his? He popped the key off his key ring and handed it to me no questions asked. I thanked him and headed across the lawn to Vickie's while he went back to raising the automotive dead.

I went around to the backdoor. I clicked open my pocket knife to cut the police tape, unlocked the door and went inside.

Street light shone through the front windows, sliced to ribbons by the Venetian blinds. I drew them shut and flicked on the light. The room felt eerily cool. It seemed empty even with all the furniture jockeying for space. If there were copies of these pictures, I hoped she had hidden them in the house. The place was cluttered; this was going to take a while. I headed into the living room.

I checked the obvious places—under the couch, in the books on the shelves, behind the framed pictures on the wall. Next would be the less-obvious places like the refrigerator or under the carpet.

I had just barely started rummaging around when a rustling in the shrubs outside the front window broke my concentration. I killed the light and copped the statue act.

The large shadow of a man was broadcast against the blinds. It faltered for a second then vanished. I ran to the front door and flung it open only to get snared in the police tape. I tripped and hit the sidewalk hard. As I started to get up something came crashing down on my head filling my eyes with flashes of bright light. I went back down. I could hear a car peeling out, but by the time I was able to look up there was nothing to make out through the blue haze of burning rubber and the streetlights' glare. Another shadow approached and stood over me. It bent down.

"You all right, officer?" the grease monkey from next door asked. "That maniac nearly ran you over."

I let the assumption of authority slide. My elbows were bloody and my shoulder hurt. Not to mention my head. I felt like I had missed the bus but it hadn't missed me. Blood was running in my eye from where my assailant had attempted to install a new part in my scalp.

"You didn't happen to get a license plate number, did you?" I asked, halfway knowing the answer I was going to get.

"Gosh, I'm sorry, officer," he said. "It was too dark and he was too fast."

The neighbor helped me to my feet. I stumbled, dizzy.

"You need medical attention," he said.

"No, I just need to use your phone."

Somebody was following me. I couldn't go home. It was time for answers.

I rang up Chapman at his office to bring him up to speed, but he was long gone.

It was time to have a talk with Rosa Lee. I rung her up and told her I was on my way, promising to explain when I got there.

Chapter 14

Rosa lived in a cozy little ranch house near Ellison Park. It was fairly secluded and backed up to the woods. I took my time driving in a round about way, making extra turns, doubling back, keeping my eyes glued to the rear view mirror, making sure I wasn't being followed. Parked in her driveway was a new, blindingly white Jaguar XK150. I pulled past it and all the way through the half circle facing the street just in case I needed to split quick. I considered leaving the motor running.

Rosa Lee was a six-foot one Brazilian Glamazon who was born Esmeralda Rosa de la Vega in Belo Horizonte. Her father was a lowlife drug pusher and part-time pimp who double-crossed the wrong people, getting Rosa's mother killed in the process. Father and his then thirteen-year-old daughter fled to America settling in New York City's Lower East Side for a new life. But Daddy simply picked up where he had left off. By age fifteen, Esmeralda was on her own and on the streets. She quickly learned that besides opening eyes, her budding beauty could open doors and wallets as well. But there always was a price to be paid and earned. She grew up fast and mean.

While working as a cigarette girl at Minsky's, the girl at the ticket booth suggested to Esmeralda she try modeling. Irving Klaw, known as The Pin-up King, was always looking for fresh talent for his mail order picture business, Movie Star News. One glimpse at the Brazilian beauty's endless gams and Klaw signed her up on the spot. She shot several serials with Klaw's sister Paula.

The titles sold hot and fast worldwide—*Esmeralda's Long and Lovely Legs*, *Brazilian Bombshell* and *Esmeralda's Dilemma,* where dressed in a lacy bra and panties along with thigh-high nylons and patent leather six-inch heeled pumps, Esmeralda struggles to escape the chair she is tied to.

Meanwhile, working at Minsky's planted the striptease seed. After getting on her knees and convincing the stage manager to give her a shot, she debuted on a mid-week matinee to a half-empty house full of rummies, reprobates and rejects of the raincoat set. Word spread fast of the dynamic, long-legged Brazilian with the delicious décolletage. A little more than a month later, she had a Friday night headline slot.

Jealousy burned hot backstage; the career girls didn't much appreciate getting upstaged by a cigarette girl. Soon after, Esmeralda changed her name to Rosa Lee and hit the road.

Rosa rose to notoriety on the carnival circuit where the fly-by-night M.O. of these traveling shows permitted the girls to push the limits. In sweaty tents across the South and Midwest, men lined up and piled in to be treated to dancing gals who had no qualms in leaving nothing to their fevered imaginations. As if her long stems weren't enough, Rosa would dare to bare it all. When a stripper pulled this, it was referred to as the blow-off. Rosa's blow-off was more of a blow-up and always resulted in a cash avalanche, but it would only work towards the end of the carnival's week-long stand as the townies' rabid word of mouth would eventually fall on puritanical ears, who would in turn inform the local constabulary. But before the sheriff could take a trip out to the carnival grounds to lower the boom, the whole affair would pull up stakes during the night and vanish.

Rosa's carny reputation preceded her once she graduated to grander, indoor stages where she was billed as The Beauty with the Brazilian Dollar Legs.

But the old bump'n'grind just got old and she hung up her G-string. I suppose there's just so much leering and latching on from lecherous Lotharios a lady can take night after night.

I'd heard word that on a stop during her last tour, one classless cad had enjoyed Rosa's act so much he began to watch with his hands. Rosa, who had a working knowledge in several unpronounceable forms of the martial arts, broke his nose with a swift kick to the face. The grabby jerk turned out to be the son of a circuit court judge and things got dicey. The situation ultimately was settled on the Q.T., but Rosa saw this as an opportunity to bow out and made her exit.

Soon after, she married a banker from Rochester who was twice her age and had caught her act while on business in Manhattan. He wasn't your run-of-the-mill stage door Johnny; he wasn't in for the typical dine and dash. He saw stars, she saw dollar signs. They were married for two years before he died of the heart attack everyone knew he'd get eventually, being married to Rosa and all.

Hubby's insurance money set her up and got her comfy, but her wild streak wouldn't let her sit still.

In the years that followed, she dabbled in photography, but the main source of her income was management and representation. In other words, she hustled.

I had caught her act years ago at The Embassy Theatre, one of the stops on the northeast burlesque wheel, over on South Avenue. The Embassy had been here forever.

Built in the mid-1800's, it was originally called the Grand Opera House and featured spectacles like Buffalo

Bill Cody's Western melodrama *The Scout of the Plains.* My older brother and I used to sneak into The Embassy through a fire door on the roof when we were teenagers. And after a surreptitious peek of Sally Rand's fan dance burned its way into the fevered fissures of my fifteen-year-old brain, I knew I'd found my calling and where I needed to go to have it answered. My innocence was left in the wake of these torrid torso-tossers' hip-shake'n'quake.

Chapter 15

As my photo skills improved, I began to incorporate and capture the same tease, tension and motion I witnessed on stage into my work. But these were qualities you couldn't just teach a model. No matter how pretty she was, if she didn't have it she wasn't going to get it. Most of the girls at The Embassy had it and the traveling acts definitely had it. One in particular was Lilly Christine, known as the Cat Girl. She had appeared in a few B-movies that went nowhere in the late 1940's before gilding the burlesque stage. Lilly was more of a belly dancer than a stripper—something she always pointed out in interviews—with an unbelievably curvaceous and tanned body and long, long bottle-blonde hair. Her performance of signature routines such as *Cat Dance*, *Voodoo Dance*, *Dance of Love* and *Harem Heat* was a mind-blowing full-on jungle drum come-on. She slinked like a panther and undulated in a vertical slither.

Based in New Orleans where she was a star attraction at Leon—Louis' brother—Prima's 500 Club, Lilly had a successful stint a couple years back in the Broadway show *Strip for Action*. She frequently traveled for sold-out performances all over Europe. And now I was going to take her picture. I couldn't stop grinning. My face was starting to hurt.

Ernie, the drummer in The Embassy house band, had met Lilly last year when the touring act he was beating the tubs for played a two-night stand at the 500 Club. He gave her a call to drop my name and put in a good word when he found out she was coming to Rochester. I was granted thirty minutes to shoot with her—Lilly Christine—in her dressing room between evening performances. I couldn't believe my luck.

Ernie was an old pal of mine. He was the cat that added some jump and thump to the onstage bump when he wasn't shooting dice. We grew up together in Irondequoit. He was constantly on the lookout for potential models to send my way. I'd always tighten him up with a couple of choice prints of whatever discovery he had hipped me to. I owed him big time on this one...real big.

I was nervous as hell the day of the shoot. I was up half the night checking my gear, going through picture scenarios in my head, and of course, laying out what I was going to wear.

This gal was in high demand and was routinely featured on the covers of magazines like *Modern Man*, *Gala*, *Vue*, *Show*, *Tempo*, *Rogue* and *Taboo* to name just a few. And though I had had my work published in the pages of some of these magazines on a semi-regular basis, Lilly Christine was essentially a shoo-in for a larger spread and a shot at the cover.

That night, Ernie walked me through the backstage labyrinth, brushing by performers on their way to or from the stage or just milling about, waiting for their cue.

After more deliberation than a teenage girl on the first day of school, I opted for a grey suit with white flecks, a two-tone open-collar shirt with a diamond pattern going down one side and cap-toe kicks. Ernie eyeballed me up and down before giving me a wink and the thumbs up.

"You look swell, man," he said as he gave me a sturdy attaboy pat on the back. He leaned forward and sniffed.

"Maybe a little heavy on the aftershave," he said with a crinkled nose. "But other than that, you're aces."

We got to the door at the end of a narrow hallway. Ernie cleared his throat and knocked.

"Mister Valentine here to see Miss Christine," he said in an official tone.

It was like a scene straight out of a movie. She opened the door in a gold silk robe that outlined her taught frame. I swear I could hear violins playing; I'm not sure if Ernie heard them or not, he was busy with the formal introductions.

"Hello, Mister Valentine," Lilly said.

"You can call me Frank," I said in a voice that didn't sound like mine. She shook my hand.

"Well then," she said. "Hello, Frank. So you'd like to take some pictures, would you?"

The room was quaint, but larger than I had imagined. It had been freshly painted light blue. Floral drapes alluded to a window that wasn't there and in the far corner stood a floor length mirror reflecting what was. Next to it sat a red velvet couch which had seen better days. Its worn expression hinted at the stories it could tell. A paint-by-numbers painting of a sad clown hung above the couch. For just a second, I thought it was a mirror. The opposite wall had a little dressing table with a lighted mirror behind it. It was cluttered with Lilly's make-up and incidentals.

She disrobed to reveal a bejeweled two-piece outfit. She effortlessly glided in high heels over to the couch, perched on the edge, crossed legs and put her hands on her breasts. We just stood there motionless.

"Shall we get started?" she asked. I set up one Fresnel light at a slight angle and parked a reflector to the side, trying to get that cool Bernard of Hollywood look. I banged out around two dozen shots when our session got cut short by the stage manager.

"Five minutes, Miss Christine," he said.

I thanked her profusely. She gave me a peck on the cheek and said I was cute. I couldn't wait to see what I had snapped in our interrupted photo session. I left the theatre right after taking in her last performance and drove over to Carl's to put the film in the overnight drop box. That way Robert would get it processed and printed first thing in the morning.

I curbed the Merc and reached in back for my camera bag. I hadn't unloaded my camera yet. Even with the windows up you could hear me yell. I let out a torrent of profanity so vile it practically melted the windshield. I had forgotten to load film into the camera.

Chapter 16

Besides the elusive Lilly Christine, there were all kinds of national talent that headlined The Embassy stage each week. Gals like Evelyn West, "The Gal With the $50,000 Treasure Chest," the six-foot eight striptease Glamazon Ricki Covette, and the "Marilyn Monroe of Burlesque"–and one of my personal favorites–Dixie Evans. However, more and more folks were staying home parked on the couch to watch television. Made-on-the-cheap burlesque films were slowly threatening theatres that featured live performers. The Embassy still brought in an enthusiastic—albeit smaller—crowd with a bevy of bodacious babes. Rosa Lee was easily one of the best. She was more than just your run-of-the-mill gams'n'gimmick fare.

She had fans rigged in the footlights that billowed soft pillars of silk up around her like smoke. Bathed in soft blue light, she swayed and undulated as smoothly and weightlessly as the sheer fabric around her. It was sexy and salacious, yet there was still plenty of sophisticated glamour and elegance. There were as many women as there were men in Rosa's audiences.

But even if she'd stood motionless, she still would have been something else to behold. Her legs went on for days and she was so stacked her bust entered the room five minutes before she did. It was like double-D in 3-D. And since she was taller than most men, they didn't need to sneak a peek at the peaks; they were already at see-level. With all this voluptuous artillery and the way she worked it, Rosa could make every part of a man sweat, drool, throb, run, pop, stiffen and ache. It was a vertical expression of horizontal desires.

There was always a pause at the end of her routine as the stunned audience came back to earth erupting in thunderous applause. Rosa always got a standing ovation—even from those who were sitting down.

This was nothing new to me; I'd been tantalized and tempted plenty of times before by all sorts of busty burlesque bar-b-que. They were almost unreal in a way. But this one, there was something more. She was captivating. I just had to meet her.

Ernie the striptease Svengali set it up.

"Jesus," he said. "She's got legs up to her neck. And that balcony...wow! Make sure you bring film this time, ya knucklehead." He was never going to let me live that down. But then again, neither was I. Ernie brought me backstage to meet Rosa where we instantly hit it off.

Ernie casually made the introductions and she took my hand in both of hers.

"Hey, Frank," he said as if the idea had just popped into his head. "Why don't you take Rosa's picture?"

He turned to Rosa who was still holding my hand.

"This guy is aces with a camera," he said. "In fact, he recently shot Lilly Christine." I glared at him and he left it at that.

She raised one eyebrow in intrigue.

"Well, I could use some new promotional slicks," she said, while looking me up and down.

"And I think I need to see what all this looks like up close," I shot back, while looking her up and down. "Professional curiosity, you understand." That's all it took.

We arranged to get together when she came through town a month or so later.

During our first session, she had taken my professionalism for indifference.

"You find me resistible?" she had asked with an exaggerated pout.

"No, no," I said. "But I'm trying to be a good boy. I don't want you to think I'm a creep. Mom taught me to be a gentleman, you know, 'please' and 'thank you,' stuff like that." There was a glint in her eye as she moved toward me like she was stalking prey. I swallowed hard. Even if I'd wanted to, there was nowhere to run. She grabbed me and pulled me into her.

"How about I please," she said. "And you say 'thank you.'"

That shoot wound up lasting three days—three of the best days of my life. She pleased and pleased and just about broke me in two until I was all out of thank you's.

A few years later she vacated the Big Apple and moved here with her husband and set up shop. New York was pricey and the services she excelled in were already offered in abundance. She could still maintain her bigger accounts from here while establishing a local branch for her in–demand services.

Once her old man took his deep-six holiday, we dated a little. I tried to keep it casual. But before long, Rosa started to get more and more serious, buying me gifts and acting increasingly jealous. She would call at all hours and she'd get upset if she found out any of her girls were seen with me. A few that had—socially or for photo shoots—mysteriously moved away or suddenly changed careers. I finally put on the brakes and she got sore. But the door was still open.

Every now and then, I'd break down and stop in for a romp, a little one-on-one; Rosa was a little hung up, but she was some pretty primo stuff. Besides, bygones were bygones, especially when a hard-on was a hard-on.

But regrettably tonight was more about the Q&A than the T&A; she was going to tell me who the mystery gentleman was...or not.

Chapter 17

The luscious Miss Lee had been waiting for me in a sheer nightgown and swung the door open swiftly, leaving me to knock air where the door had been. It wasn't really a nightgown but more like a suggestion, a nightgown's shadow. It was as opaque as the steam rising up from my collar. The warm glow of the room bordered her fine frame like a full body halo accentuated by the smoke of her cigarette. The lady smoked Ladyfingers—ultra-expensive, ultra-thin feminine smokes right down to their pale pink wrapper and gold band, imported from somewhere exotic in the Far East. She held a drink in one hand as she extended the other to me, giving me a look that could've been poured on waffles. The seduction left her face when she saw the dried blood on mine. She reached to touch it.

"Oh, you're hurt," she said.

"I'll be okay," I said, backing up. "I just need to talk to you. I think I'm in some trouble." I didn't want to let on what I knew. I wanted to see what she wanted me to know.

"Come in, handsome," she said like a spider to a fly. "Let me get a better look at you."

Rosa led me to the sunken lounge encircled by a zebra print couch and various oversized pillows. In the center was an active fire pit, its dancing demons cackled, crackled and glowed. It was a swank pad, pleasant and plush, just like its statuesque proprietress. She was beautiful and she knew it, too. Large black and white prints and show bills from her tenure in the daily bump'n'grind dominated the walls alongside some of her own photography. They were mostly of girls I recognized from her own stable, including one of Vickie Hayes. It was a beautiful shot. Out of the corner of my eye, I noticed her noticing me noticing it.

"Nice shot," I said. "It's a shame..." I trailed off. Rosa said nothing.

I was trying to warm up and into the questions, but genuinely meant what I said. It was a nice shot.

Rosa was a good photographer. She had an eye for it made keen by years on the other side of the lens as well as the benefit of seeing her subjects unencumbered by libido. Florida-based photographer Bunny Yeager was another good example of this. All Yeager's shots exhibited a trust and a genuine playfulness as the model splashed and romped uninhibited and free. Male photographers always had an element of seduction to contend with—for better or for worse. Not every model wants to get hit on, but not every photographer wants to bed the model. For me, well, that depends on the circumstances. I'm flexible.

There's also the romantic insight most women possess making men painfully transparent. Women see women in an entirely different light. They can also read men's minds when it comes to their competition, or more simply put, any other woman in the room. A woman can take one look at another and tell instinctively, and immediately, what her man wants to do with her or what he has already done with her. I don't care how poker you can make your face, how dead you can get your pan, once you're a blip on their radar screen there isn't any getting around it, beyond it, past it or out of it. We're all guilty of something.

Her eyes narrowed when I pressed her about Vickie. She zeroed in on me.

"Why?" she asked pointedly. "You liked her, didn't you?"

It was none of her business. I denied it, but she knew.

She stared back at me.

"Would you stop it? It was strictly professional," I said. "Just a model I hired for some portfolio work."

She folded her arms and took a sharp, angry drag off her pink cigarette.

"So you always bring flowers to a professional shoot?" she asked, playing with the words like an eight-year-old brat.

"Just trying to be...hey!"

She had followed me again.

"Honey, this has got to stop. We've been over this. It ain't ever gonna happen, especially when you're spying on me. It's really not an attractive quality. Now, who was this guy she was with?"

"I don't know what you're talking about."

So this was how she was going to play it. She kept with the dumb routine when I mentioned Donovan's name as well. She wasn't going to give up a damn thing.

I had three problems: the killer, Donovan and Hayes. Donovan wasn't necessarily interested in finding the real killer; he was content in seeing me hang. And Hayes was gonna go at this with the sensitivity of a battering ram. I put my head in my hands and muttered to myself. Rosa shifted gears.

"You can stay here if you like, if you want to lay low," she said. "I'll take care of you."

"I can't lay low," I said. "I've got to find out who killed this girl before Donovan hangs the rap on me or Hayes puts me in orthopedic shirts."

"You don't need to do anything right now. I need to do something..." She stood up...and kept standing up. I'd dated entire women as tall as her legs. She let her nightgown slowly slip off her shoulders. I pushed her aside and onto the couch. She protested with a "harrumph" as I made for the door. I had to get the hell out of there before I changed my mind. My groin—and the rest of my body for that matter—joined in with the throbbing in my head. I was one big thundering pulse. I hightailed it back to the casbah and filled the bathtub with ice. I sat in it until it melted.

Chapter 18

Tossing and twisting the sheets into knots, searching in vain for a cool spot on the bed, I couldn't sleep. When my eyelids got too heavy and I'd get close, I'd see Vickie but I couldn't run to her. Or I'd see her father or Donovan and couldn't run away from them.

It was 4 a.m. when I gave up. So I decided to go back to Vickie's and look for the photos some more. Hopefully, I'd beat out whoever was looking to get their grubby paws on them.

I dumped the car on the street a block from Vickie's and hoofed it quickly through a couple back yards, setting off a canine chorus in my wake. Backyard lights were being flicked on and dogs were still being told to shut up as I pried a back window open. I pulled myself into the bathroom. No need to bother with the lights this time; I had a flashlight.

I hit the bedroom first. I could still smell the faint lilac sweetness of Vickie's perfume. I began to rummage through every drawer, lingering in the lingerie briefly, before I stopped short and took a good look around. The room had already been tossed. I headed cautiously to the living room. It was wrecked.

Somebody had definitely been here since my last visit, somebody who was searching for something—and not carefully either. The place had been ransacked. It looked like a bomb had gone off. Books and knickknacks had been knocked off the shelves, odds and ends had been upended and furniture had been flipped over with its pillows and cushions gutted. The searcher's desperation was apparent as virtually everything had been turned upside down and inside out. The search appeared frantic and thorough, but hopefully not fruitful.

I scoured the joint anyway—under furniture, in the light fixtures, in cushions. Nothing.

Behind pictures, under shelves and in all the books. More nothing.

As I headed for the kitchen, I stumbled over the portable record player on the floor, knocking over the stack of records we had played the night we had shot pictures. Right on top was her favorite: Martin Denny's *Exotica* with a dozen or so black and white prints and a plastic sleeve of negatives peaking out of the record cover. Bingo.

I held the flashlight in my teeth and quickly thumbed through the shots. I sat down at the kitchen table. Oh boy, this was major league. I recognized the face right away from his campaign flyers: Judge Preston Jenkins, Family First. This cat was a political and social bigwig. But here he was as Vickie's co-star in a decidedly decadent display.

Known to all as a man's man—ordinarily—here Jenkins was dolled up in full make-up, a bustier, stockings, heels and a blonde wig. He was having his way with a saucy brunette in drag—in this case, Vickie Hayes in a little tuxedo coat, top hat and a drawn on mustache. She looked thoroughly satisfied as the photo scenario progressed from sublime and somewhat choreographed to up close and explicit. As far as I could tell, other than the swapped outfits, it was stock one-on-one pornography. That is before I got to the shots where roles got reversed and the saucy judge wound up being violated himself. It was raunchy as hell. I rubbed my eyes and let out a little chuckle before I remembered the price that had been paid for these snaps so far. And it was far from being paid in full.

Now I could see why these might cost a few bucks, hell, maybe even a few lives. Jenkins had enough juice to collect on both counts. I got the hell out of Vickie's pad the same way I had come in with the record sleeve full of political dynamite and stashed it safely in the car. Sure, some of my questions had been addressed. I just wasn't expecting these answers. I was a long way from breathing easy. My head hurt. I couldn't think. My stomach growled low and mean. It was probably a good idea to feed it something before it turned on me.

Chapter 19

The morning sky glowed cherry red as I pulled up to the diner just down the street from Rosa's. I had called Chapman and he agreed to meet me there. I'd kill some time here and go back to her pad for round two of the questioning.

The pre-dawn cool offered temporary relief from what promised to be another scorcher. Chapman was already seated at the far end of the crowded counter when I strolled in.

"Good morning, handsome," Louise said, as she poured my coffee.

"It is now," I said.

An eyeful of Louise would further breakfast's resuscitation so I could concentrate and get to the bottom of all that had happened...or get out from under it. The cast of characters was growing, yet what each person's role in this charade—including mine—was, wasn't clear just yet.

I managed a grin and winked at Louise as I straddled my stool. There were plenty of booths open, where a guy could spread the paper out and sit comfortably, but me, I liked to sit at the counter and watch Louise work. Apparently so did everyone else—most mornings the counter was packed elbow to elbow. Silverware clinked and clanked amidst a mish-mash of conversations. Guys going to work, guys just getting off work, old men pontificating all sat at the counter enjoying the scenery. She was particularly gorgeous this morning. A few of her fans at the counter were going to be late for work.

Maybe it was the way she walked the narrow aisle behind the counter, her hips swinging as if in slow motion no matter how fast she moved. Maybe it was her gorgeous smile and those marmalade eyes sparkling beneath waves of scrambled yellow hair. Maybe it was the way she spilled out of her uniform whenever she'd lean in to top off your coffee. It could be steak and eggs or simply a coffee and danish, either way we were all eating out of Louise's hand.

"Judge Preston Jenkins," I said to Chapman.

"Huh?" he said.

"The guy in the pictures. Judge Preston Jenkins."

Chapman took the napkin out of his lap and stood up. He looked pale.

"I gotta go," he said. "I'll be in touch."

I set to work on a big breakfast like a condemned man, pausing every few bites to take in the floor show. I was halfway through my eggs when I heard it.

You work with law enforcement long enough you get used to the sounds. The crackle of a police radio. The leather utility belt rattle and squeak all beat cops had. And the sound of an intercept motor.

The first cruiser blew by with a roar. It was when the second and then the third followed that I took notice. Something was up. Something big. I dialed dispatch from the pay phone by the door.

"What's the hub-bub, darlin'?" I asked. "The cavalry just came through with a quickness."

Louise looked up as I dropped the phone. It swung on its cord and bounced off the wall with a crack. I stood there for a moment, stunned.

"What's the matter, honey?" she asked.

Her question hung in the air as I flung a couple crumpled bills on the counter and flew out the door. I peeled out of the parking lot, fishtailing into the street to a litany of screeching tires and angry horns. I pounded the steering wheel and shouted at the windshield.

"No, no, no, no..."

I drove like a maniac, all the way back to Rosa's house.

Chapter 20

Pandemonium greeted me as I slid into her driveway behind the black and whites. But it was nothing compared to the circus inside. Uniform cops were running everywhere, shouting. I ran to the house picking up fractured bits of what was going on.

"She put up one helluva fight."

"She must've put a hurtin' on the bastard for sure."

"You know who she is, don't you?"

"Boy, did you get a load of those legs?"

As I made my way to the door I was pushed back by a surge of blue uniforms flanking several white ones.

"Make way, make way," they shouted. "Comin' through."

Paramedics were rolling Rosa out on a gurney. Her face was bruised and her hair matted with blood. She had a fat lip and her left eye was swollen shut. She was a mess, but she was alive.

I was beginning to feel like a pariah. This was my fault.

She looked up at me and tried to smile.

"Honey, I'm sorry," I said.

A heavy hand came down on the back of my neck.

"You're goddamn right you're sorry," Donovan said. "Arrest this scum bag."

Chapter 21

Two metal chairs and a table were the only things keeping me company in the little ten-by-ten interview room located in the bowels of the headquarters building downtown. They weren't at all comfortable and seemed to contour everywhere the human body didn't. But then again, if you found yourself sitting in here, they could be plush velvet recliners and you'd still be on edge. This was the hot seat.

All of the furniture teetered crookedly. The institution gray paint had been worn off the chair's arms by years of handcuffs and fingernails. My employment had afforded me some consideration and I wasn't restrained, but I was still in a tight spot. I folded my arms and put them on the table. It was covered with drink rings and slime, and my sweaty skin stuck. The whole room mirrored my situation—bleak. And it was beginning to feel more like nine-by-nine.

This was the stage where detectives exercised a little persuasion—good cop/bad cop, bad cop/bad cop. It was a theatre of broken rules and broken ribs. Guys like Donovan did their best work here. The lighting flickered intermittently. A paper cup filled with water—a token gesture of hospitality—just sat there soggy and untouched, bathed in as much condensation as I was.

There were deep grooves gouged into the dingy linoleum and the walls were freckled with tiny brown dots. It was affectionately known as "The Confessional." The Confessional was sinister, silent, soundproofed.

My lies had not only complicated my involvement, but had gotten Rosa hurt. Obviously, whoever had been following me didn't care who they put the hurt or the blame on. Neither did Donovan, even though he was putting on a good show as if he did. If I had just simply 'fessed up in the first place, I wouldn't be here in this mess expected to spill my guts. I didn't kill anybody, damn it. But now I had to see this thing through...after I got clear of Donovan.

Donovan came in with another man I didn't recognize. This guy was huge, a regular giant with bad skin, Sasquatch in a cheap suit. His whole frame filled the doorway so he had to stoop to clear it. He didn't look like a cop. He was the dark and handsome type that was only handsome when it was dark. I couldn't read this bruiser; he just stared, blankly. Donovan, on the other hand, was smiling. I'm not sure which mug was more unsettling. The room was starting to squeeze.

Eight-by-eight and counting.

He slid the other chair out and sat down in front of me. He rolled up his sleeves, stretched out his hairy arms before him and cracked his knuckles. They were rough and bloody. This wasn't his first tune-up of the day. I really didn't want to be there.

"Looks like she got a coupla licks in, too," he said to Sasquatch, pointing at the gash above my eyebrow. "You gonna tell me what happened?" I knew where this was headed but I still pulled the iceberg act. I had nothing to lose except maybe some teeth...maybe a little blood.

"I cut myself shaving," I said as cool and as deadpan as possible. Maybe they would admire my guts.

Maybe not.

The giant punched me in them instead and I fell forward out of my seat and into Donovan.

"Keep bumpin' your gums," he said. "There's more where that came from."

He shoved me back into my chair. I wheezed like a busted accordion, trying to catch my breath.

"You were there, shitbird, I know it," he said. I tried the crazy act and dished out a little delirium.

"Not being informed of the true path of recognition," I said with a smirk. "I feel a delicacy in articulating for fear of deviating from the true path of rectitude." It was a phrase I'd picked up after a night of heavy drinking with some trapeze artists who were here in town with the circus. After each drink, we'd recite it until it made no sense.

It made no sense to these two gorillas either, but it bought me a few moments peace.

"What the hell does that mean?" Donovan said, looking at Sasquatch. Sasquatch said nothing and clobbered me with a phonebook in the side of the head instead. This was an old trick that, when done correctly, never left incriminating bruises or welts after a heated interrogation. I shook my poor *cabeza*, trying to get rid of the little stars that had begun to appear. The room was approaching six-by-six and getting a little hazy. I swallowed hard.

"I'm telling you...I didn't...do this," I said.

"What about the Hayes broad? Why were you there last night snooping around if you...?" He caught himself a little too late. I had most of my wind back, and my guts. I got loud.

"Son of a bitch," I said. "You were outside her house." We both stood up. "So you're in on this caper, too, aren't you? You're trying to set me up."

His eyes told me I was onto something. He grabbed my shirt and jammed me up against the wall. He was foaming at the mouth.

"Where are those pictures?"

A-ha! Confirmation. Affirmation. Vindication. I knew it. The playing field had just been leveled a bit, even if Donovan had the home court advantage. He lowered his voice and repeated himself slowly.

"Where...are...those ...pictures?" he asked.

"Why don't you ask your friend Mike Conway?"

Sasquatch spoke up for the first time.

"It's funny," he said. "You bringing up a dead man's name." Donovan looked confused again.

"For the last time," he said, "the pictures, Valentine."

I winked at Sasquatch. He was barely paying attention, just waiting his turn to apply more of the treatment.

"Which ones?" I asked. "The ones of your wife?" It just slipped out. When was I gonna learn? The same sense of humor that used to get me out of tough situations was now getting me into them. Donovan let me down. He smoothed my shirt, patted me on the shoulder and smiled. He turned as if to walk away then turned back as if he had one more thing to say.

It was what the old boxers call a telegraph punch; you can see it coming from a mile away. The problem is it often lands quicker than you think and it's lights out before you even hit the canvas.

Chapter 22

Haunted by more fractured dreams: Rosa's bloody face, models in full rigor, running on lead legs from Eddie Hayes, Donovan's breath, photographing Lilly Christine with no film in the camera...

I woke up on the floor of the tiny holding cell reserved for drunks to sleep it off. I had been put to bed with a shovel, at least it felt that way. I had two roommates, one was sawing logs loudly in a puddle of drool, the other was slouched against the wall. He looked dead.

"Valentine. Hey you, Valentine." The voice reverberated as if from the bottom of a very deep well. It was the morning shift-change with lots of coming and going. My cell was unlocked and a young guard with a crooked grin, and an equally crooked haircut he had obviously given himself, was looking down at me. He didn't know my story but his eyes confirmed my presumed guilt. Good guys don't just wind up in jail. Everybody's guilty of something. My eyes started to shut again on their own and he kicked my foot.

"You're free to go," he said. "Prescott wants to see you first."

I was sure there would be no record of my visit with Donovan. It hadn't been an official interview; I was never really under arrest...technically. They had cuffed me at Rosa's but I hadn't been checked in with the desk sergeant. I could have been locked up down here for days or very easily disappeared permanently and nobody would've ever known.

Old timers like Donovan were given a lot of latitude as long as bad guys got caught and crimes got solved. It made the brass happy and made for good press. And when these guys went outside the law to enforce it, everybody seemed to be looking the other way. The smart ones anyway.

On the surface, I was gumming up the works on Donovan's investigation. He and I both knew I was closing in on something shady. The question was, was Donovan basking in that shade? The fact he hadn't arrested me or dragged me further into the investigation pointed at his own involvement somehow. Perhaps he was worried I had something on him. And maybe I did. Yet, on the off chance he was on the up-and-up and truly trying to solve this case—which I doubted very much—there was no way I was going to tip him off or help him out. Rossi? I'd help Rossi, sure. Donovan? Hell no.

Other than exhibiting some poor judgment and sitting on some info, I had done nothing wrong. There was nothing I could be charged with. But Prescott was gonna be sore with me. My job was in jeopardy.

I took a birdbath in the men's room, congratulating my inconsistency in the mirror—not bad, I didn't look as rotten as I felt. I headed upstairs to Prescott's office. I could hear two loud voices going at it through the closed door. One voice was the captain's. The other I didn't recognize, but it clearly belonged to somebody who was hot and bothered.

"I want to know just what the hell you're doing about it," he was saying as I knocked. Prescott grunted an invite and I walked into the storm.

Prescott was behind his desk, Eddie Hayes was in front. Both men were standing. The air was electric and tense. Hayes pointed a big finger at me, the other four made a formidable fist.

"Is this the guy?" he asked. I took a step back and looked at Prescott to try and gauge how soon the big fist and my face were going to meet.

The captain made the introductions. I reached out my hand to Hayes, not really expecting him to take it. He didn't. Instead, he pointed to Prescott's desk.

"You take these pictures?" Hayes asked.

No matter how much you're exposed to the female figure, it still grabs you and gives you a start. That initial, flesh-induced thrill never gets old. There were a dozen or so nude shots spread out over Prescott's desk, pictures of full-blown voluptuosity in beautiful black and white. The pictures I had taken of Vickie and some other random cheesecake stuff, including a few I had snapped of Rosa a while back. Pictures of two girls—one who had since been beaten up, and one who had since wound up dead. Donovan must've gotten these out of my car. The ones he was looking for—the blackmail shots with Vickie and the judge—were noticeably absent; the big dummy hadn't thought to look under the spare in the wheel well.

Hayes' query hung in the air for what seemed like an eternity. I finally broke the silence.

"Yeah, I took them," I said. "So what?" Perhaps I was a little too cocky. It had worked great so far, why stop now?

Hayes lunged at me before Prescott could intercede.

"Hey, Eddie, don't," Prescott said, coming around his desk in a hurry.

I made for the door, but Hayes was too fast and slammed it shut with his meaty paw. I grabbed the flagpole by the door and swung wildly, trying to fend him off. He grabbed it and a tug of war ensued. If he got anywhere near me, he was going to kill me. His face was red and the veins in his neck were throbbing to the surface. He was furiously mashing words together through clenched teeth, trying to come up with new ways to accurately express his anger much in the way my old man used to when the lawnmower wouldn't start. Every spring I would marvel as Dad would beautifully blend profanity, vulgarity and Sicilian slang into a potent and putrid parlance. It was both shockingly crude and eloquent. Sometimes plain old profanity didn't do the trick.

Hayes had lost a daughter, no father wants that. And he was now facing the man who had inadvertently alerted him to the fact that his little girl now had big girl parts. No father wants that, either.

His anger made him even stronger than he already was and I wound up against the wall with the flagpole up under my chin. It seemed I was spending a lot of time with my back up against the wall lately. We were face to face. My feet were off the ground. I wondered when, if ever, Prescott was going to step in, another eternity. I couldn't breathe. I began to black out. It doesn't hurt as much when your lights are out.

I was hunched over with my hands on my knees, choking and gasping for air as Prescott and two other officers were talking to Hayes. It had taken three of them to peel him off of me. I slid down the wall to the floor rubbing my throat and seriously considering a career change.

Wedding photography, I thought. Yeah, wedding photography. Or babies, even.

"Eddie," Prescott was saying. "You've got to let us do our job, pal. This isn't helping." Hayes kicked the wall next to my head and I flinched as the paneling crunched. He was still glaring at me, fuming. So was the Captain.

I could have argued until I was blue in the face, but I knew when Prescott got my formerly withheld info, at best, a suspension was coming. At worst I'd be out on my ass. At least I wasn't in jail. But now the situation wasn't as clear-cut, a judge and a cop were mixed up in it. Who knew what that was exactly and who had what to gain was becoming more and more unclear. Still, I had to say something. I rubbed my neck, stalling for time. I stood up cautiously.

Prescott pulled the old confessor trick—stand there and say absolutely nothing. The silence will gnaw at a guilty conscience until rats rat, guts spill and canaries sing. I was wise to the maneuver, but still had something to say. Besides, I was innocent...essentially. I glanced over at Hayes, he seemed to have cooled down some. I stayed by the wall just in case.

"Captain," I said, "Donovan's connected to this somehow and he's setting me up on account of his wife," I protested. "It's a personal beef." Prescott was unmoved. I continued, a little louder.

"A girl's dead, her killer's still out there and Donovan's wasting everybody's time with this bullshit." Still nothing.

I looked over to Hayes, probably not the best place to look for an ally.

"Look, man," I said, "she was my friend." He just glared back at me. "She was a swell kid, but I think she got mixed up in some bad business that went worse. I think I can get to the bottom of this if you guys would just give me a little wiggle room. This is a world where you guys will stick out like a hooker at a garden party. They—whoever they are—will see you coming."

I reiterated my advantage.

"This is where I do my thing," I said.

The room seemed to relax for a minute. They were actually listening to me. I threw out a little teaser.

"Look, there're pictures out there to prove it. They may implicate some pretty important people. Hell, the DOA by the river was a PI looking for these same pictures and look what happened to him. If I'm right about Donovan, it'll mean egg on your face, too, Captain."

Hayes cut in, deflated.

"I've already seen enough goddamn pictures," he said.

Hayes had heard enough, too. He slumped into a chair next to Prescott's desk. He hung his head down shaking it from side to side. He groaned.

"My poor little girl," he said. He was quieter now, defeated and heartbroken. But as long as his fists remained clenched, I couldn't relax. I wasn't going to present the pictures right away. I'd get them to Rossi once I had a few more answers that didn't include my name. No, I'd hold on to these pictures for the time being. Hayes was in no big hurry anyhow. And I certainly didn't need him seeing these. He'd kill me for sure.

Prescott remained silent with his arms still folded. He acknowledged the photos on his desk by not acknowledging the photos on his desk. More cop psychology. He was breathing hard through his nostrils. He was a volcano about to blow.

I already had the pictures and though Mickey was loosely involved, I was pretty sure I could count on him as a witness. And if I could get Donovan's ex to come clean on the affair that never was, it would hopefully deflate his vendetta some or at least cool down some of its supporters. But there was a new snag; he knew I was onto him. I shared my plan of attack with the captain.

"All right," I said with a renewed sense of get-up and can-do. "I'll prove it. I'm gonna go talk to some of these people, track down these photos, get Donovan's old lady to clear this up. That way you can concentrate on the real crime here." There it was. It sounded perfectly logical to me. I had appointed myself in charge.

That did it.

Mount Prescott finally blew its top—so loud it even startled Hayes.

"You stay away from Donovan and his wife," he shouted. "You're on suspension, Valentine. You hear me?" But I was already out the door. I could hear Hayes start up his word search again as I made my way down the hall posthaste.

I stopped by a wall phone and got an outside line. I dialed Conway Private Investigations and the girl put me through.

Chapter 23

"You left in a hurry," I said on the phone to Chapman. "Everything copasetic?" Chapman sounded grave.

"The business is broke," he said. "Busted, gutted, finished, washed up."

He went on for about five minutes. Money embezzled, money gambled, money gone, betrayal, shattered trust. Collection notices had been piling up unbeknownst to him. And now what little he found out about Conway's involvement with the judge was hinky as well.

"Gee, you think he was in on it?" I asked.

"It looks like it," he said. "There're recordings here you ought to listen to."

"Of what?"

"A conversation. Conway and Jenkins. Jenkins doesn't sound too happy. He sounds desperate to get his hands on these pictures. I've searched Mike's office and haven't found a goddamn thing. Maybe he was bluffing, Christ, I don't know."

I had a stop to make but promised I'd be at his office shortly.

Out of the pressure cooker and into the summertime heat. I was already out to the parking lot and fishing around in my pants pocket for my keys, when I realized my car was still in Rosa's driveway. Tooling around in something that conspicuous probably wasn't such a hot idea anyway. I hailed a cab and had him drive me over to Donovan's ex-wife's pad instead.

Chapter 24

Gail Gifford Donovan lived in a plush pad in a swank apartment building on East Avenue, just a few blocks outside downtown. Walking through the gilded doors pretty much confirmed my suspicions about Donovan; there's no way alimony from a straight cop's salary could've ever covered this rent. Even though she came from money, it had already been spent. The wealth was long gone, but Gail still lived as if the gravy train was still on the rails.

It was a grand old building built at the turn of the century. The main foyer was pink and gray marble with a well worn, formerly red carpet down the middle. The elevator had elaborate brass deco doors that yawned slowly as I approached. I got in and punched the number five. It was old and slow so I took the opportunity to close my eyes as it took its sweet time creaking and groaning up to the fifth floor.

Gail was a debutante who fell—or dove—from grace. She came from old money that cringed at her party girl behavior. Her grandfather, John Gifford, had laid the initial nest egg in the stock market before the crash. Her father, John, Jr., floundered in the old man's footsteps; he didn't have his stock market savvy or financial acumen, but they were so loaded it would be years until the money ran out. They looked rich, they acted rich, but the blue blood was slowly bleeding out. Dad kept up appearances, Mom stayed drunk. They had three beautiful girls, two of which successfully married off into obscurity.

Thanks in part to Gail—not to mention her father's ineptitude—the Gifford family wound up on the fast track to the skids and her father blew his brains out with a shotgun in front of the whole family during Thanksgiving dinner.

Gail was the youngest and the one with the wild streak. She started out on top, captain of the cheerleading squad at West Irondequoit High School, honor roll, dean's list, scholarship to Penn State and so on. She seemed to be on the right track, but boys and booze derailed her. By the time she first met Donovan she was twenty years old with a foul mouth and a classy chassis and had been working as a high-end call girl for several years. It was during a routine roundup for the department's semi-annual prostitution sting when he worked vice. She had persuaded him to let her slide for trade and before too long, things escalated. With a cop on her arm, she could get away with things even Daddy's money couldn't buy her out of. And with her on his arm...well, physically he was way, way, way out of his league.

Gail and Donovan's mutually beneficial charade carried on for a while and wound up with a stroll down the aisle. They lived the high life for a little while after that, but her tastes and habits were expensive. She'd simply had too many good times with too much and too many for too long to settle for just one with a meager public servant's salary, a beer gut and whiskey dick.

It had been a blur and barely a year when she gave her meal ticket a one-way ticket on the *adios* express. That was right about the time she hired me to take some risqué boudoir shots of her—to feel better about herself I suppose, but moreover to stick it to Donovan. I had done this plenty of times before for eager girlfriends and wives who wanted to pour a little gas on the home fires with a surprise for their man. But Mrs. Donovan's time in my viewfinder was definitely vindictive. Her sexuality was forced and harsh. It came off corrosive and more out of spite than anything else. But I was able to manage. She looked fabulous undressed.

We had shot at my loft studio one evening where she was volatile, pretty and pretty out of control. The vodka and pills didn't help. She flirted and flashed during the entire session and when I didn't bite, she laid it out. By the look on her face, I was the first one to ever tell her "no." Not just because she was a cop's wife, but because she looked and acted like a whole lot of trouble. Tempting, just not worth the hassle. I wasn't necessarily trying to be a good boy, but a smart one. She ended the night passed out on my couch, untouched with whatever was left of her virtue intact.

But what does she go and do? She went ahead and told Donovan we'd made it after the session anyway. The thing was, I never went out of my way to deny it. Now, it was really beginning to catch up to me.

The elevator door slid open with a dull ding shattering my thirty seconds of solace.

It was a little before noon and she answered the door, drunk. She was thrilled to see me.

"Frankie, my Valentine," she slurred loudly. "Where ya been, lover boy?"

"Oh, here and there," I said. "Gail, I need to talk to you."

"Of course you do," she said.

Her dressing gown fell open as she leaned into me for a hug. The ice clinked clumsily in her liquid lunch and it sloshed and splashed over the side. It obviously wasn't her first cocktail, or her second.

She had recently been in the sun as the tan lines on her bronzed body showed where a tiny two-piece had barely been. The goodies that hadn't seen the sun glowed a luminous white. Tan lines—one of the things that drove me crazy. She looked both delicious and dilapidated, a beautiful bleach blonde train wreck. I didn't know whether to feel bad for her or feel her up. Despite all the grief she'd caused me, I was still warm for her form. It was pretty clear she'd offer no resistance. Her eyelids did all they could do to stay open. She set her drink down in the air next to an end table and it smashed on the floor.

"Oops," she said, laughing. "Man down." She turned her attention to me. "Come here, you."

Gail threw her arms around my neck and tried to kiss me on the mouth. She missed. It caught me off balance and she yanked me inside, slamming the door behind us. She pushed me up against the wall. She was hot to trot.

"Look," I said as she covered my face with sloppy kisses and day-old lipstick. "You've gotta come clean with your old man."

"Ex-old man," she said.

"Whatever. He's making my life a living hell." She kept kissing at me, pawing at me, fumbling with my belt. Her breath smelled flammable. It was getting me drunk.

Sometimes in these situations, your body will bargain with you in order to justify what it wants. Mine just focused on her body and eliminated all concern for the baggage and physical danger associated with a chick as crazy as this one. All systems were go, on deck, in the chute gate, and I started justifying my urge to give in. I came to my senses long enough to grab her shoulders and shake her.

"Look, goddammit," I said. "Listen to me. You need to tell him nothing happened."

She shrugged off her gown, turned around and ground her backside into what would've been my lap if I'd been sitting down. Her hands were all over me.

"But something could happen now," she said turning to face me. "Perhaps you could be persuaded."

"No way. I've already got enough worry. I'm not interested."

She reached in my pants and took hold. Her eyes got big.

"I thought you weren't interested," she said as my trousers hit the floor.

I immediately changed my mind. Who knows? Maybe it would change hers.

Chapter 25

I cabbed it over to the Powers Building and took the elevator to the third floor. It was after hours, but the door was ajar. Chapman had left it open for me. The receptionist desk was neat and orderly with a vase of wilting flowers on it. All the blinds had been pulled down.

The air was cool and I caught a whiff of something burning with a chemical, acrid scent. I called out to Chapman. Nothing. I walked down the hall and peered in a few office doors. Nothing.

I got to the door with a gold plaque that said *Anthony Chapman* on it. I knocked on the partially open door. I waited a few seconds and let myself in. In the middle of the floor was a smoldering pile of ashes and melted plastic. It had stopped burning but I could tell by the shapes remaining, it had been several reel-to-reel tapes. Chapman was sitting at his desk wide-eyed with a surprised expression made permanent by a huge gash in his head.

Chapter 26

Detective Rossi cornered me in the hall the next morning.

"Heard you went head to head with Hayes," he said.

"Yeah," I said. "Apparently standing conscious on my own two feet isn't thrilling enough." Rossi let out half a laugh then went back to the stern concern.

"You're pissing off a lot of people around here, kid," he said. "What's going on?"

I told him—the judge, the pictures, Donovan, everything. After I was done, he scratched his chin thoughtfully and just stared at me for a moment.

"And you have these pictures?" he asked.

"That's just it, Ange. That's all I've got."

"Let me look into this...meanwhile you keep your nose clean."

Chapter 27

Despite the ocean of chaos I was drowning in, I still had a job to do. I didn't take Prescott's suspension seriously. Sure, I had pissed him off, but part of his reaction was merely showboating for Eddie Hayes. He couldn't get rid of me; there weren't that many of us to do this job. I found a pay phone to check in and was immediately dispatched: two stiffs, no details. My heap was still at Rosa's and since I didn't want to go over there smelling like Gail—scotch, cigarettes and Chanel—it was taxi time again. Actually, it wasn't that bad. I was getting used to being chauffeured around.

Bad news and all that leads up to it doesn't know how to take a day off. I could certainly use the distraction of someone else's misery, I thought. However, I changed my tune when I arrived at the scene: a little weather-beaten bungalow in Charlotte. There were two fire trucks as big as the house and a gas company rig out front. There was smoke and the smell of gas as I entered through the back door and into the kitchen. All the windows were open, but the putrid gas smell was still fairly prevalent. A young woman in a floral print dress and a frilly apron lay dead on the floor. There was smoke still coming from the oven, though the officers on the scene had turned it off. The roast was ruined.

"Gas leak," one of them said to me. "The gas man cut it off outside." We all looked down at the body.

"She never saw it coming," I said.

The other uniform chimed in.

"Neither did he," he said.

"He?"

"Yeah. The hubby's in there." He pointed through the door to the tiny living room. A fat man sat in a worn recliner with his hairy arms folded across his chest, his head tipped back, his mouth wide open. The morning edition was on his lap open to the local page. Another spread about Vickie. I couldn't escape it.

The kitchen was still a little hazy so I started with the living room. I got to work as the two cops went through the motions, haphazardly securing the scene while waiting for the investigators to arrive. But there seemed to be no mystery here. Accidental and tragic—it seemed pretty cut and dry.

The room was homey and quaint with a couple of recliners—the one occupied by the deceased, the other with a knitting basket sitting next to it—a couple of floor lamps and a couch against the wall opposite a small fireplace. Assorted photos stared back from its mantle. The pictures were so old it was a safe bet none of their subjects were still alive. All of their faces were appropriately grave.

The whole scene was cluttered and tight and I had to back up in order to fill the frame in my viewfinder. As I did, I backed into the gas heating unit against the wall, kicking something with a heavy clink. It was a monkey wrench, lying next to the gas line coming up through the floor. The coupling had been unscrewed and the two ends were disconnected. This is where the gas got in to this couple's house; this is where their exit made an entrance.

"Boy, doesn't that beat all?" one of the cops asked when I brought it to their attention. "Who do you suppose done it?" There were two obvious choices.

We all looked over at the stiff in the chair.

"Maybe he couldn't take it anymore."

"Maybe he just got bored," the other said. "Or maybe she did it. Either way, it's a raw deal. They both appear to have been in the middle of something. It looks like a happy home, doesn't it? Maybe it was an accident." I looked at the unscrewed gas line with raised eyebrows.

"You really think so?" I asked.

I picked up a velvet throw pillow off the worn couch. "Love" was embroidered on it, along with little hearts.

"You never know with some people," I said, tossing the pillow back on the couch. "Sometimes love isn't enough."

I took some shots of the hijacked gas line and made quick work of capturing the kitchen scene. I had to get out of there soon. The leftover gas had re-ignited my headache.

Murder, murder-suicide... either way it meant they'd have to get the Homicide dicks in on it. Which probably meant Donovan and that meant me out the door and on to the next tragedy. I waved as I made my exit.

"*Adios*," I said.

"Wait..." one of them said. I turned around to look at him. His face had gone white.

"Aww, Christ," said the other as we raced down the hall to the tiny bedroom at the end. Just inside the door, the officer was standing silently, looking down into the little crib at the foot of the bed. Sometimes love isn't enough.

Chapter 28

They had patched Rosa up and sent her home. She was pretty shaken and bruised up a bit but would recover.

I had Mickey drop me off at her pad.

"Jeez, what happened to your ride, man?" he asked as we pulled up to my car. "Looks like your baby needs a new pair of shoes."

Sure did—my baby was still parked out front, listing low with four flat shoes. And I was pretty sure she had a windshield the last time I checked. I let out a sigh.

"It's a work in progress," I said. "With a few ongoing setbacks."

"Who woulda done this?" he asked.

"The list is growing, Mick." I got out and waved him off.

The interior was a wreck as well, papers strewn about and it smelled like the men's room at Silver Stadium after a double-header. Even Lula, my lucky dashboard hula girl, had been smashed, reduced to two legs and a spring. I immediately popped the trunk and checked under the spare and breathed a little easier when I felt the record sleeve with the envelope in it—the pictures were still there.

I rang the bell twice before Rosa came to the door. She pulled aside the curtain and peered through the bars in the little window, relaxing her frown when she saw that it was me. She swung the door open and hugged me silently while shooting a nervous glance over my shoulder. She quickly pulled me inside and locked the door.

I phoned the auto club as she fixed us both a drink.

The place had been cleaned up and there was no evidence of the assault except for a hole punched in the wall by the door and the cracked glass on one of her large photographs. There were a few chairs missing.

She lit one of her pink cigarettes and sat down on the couch. She leaned back and crossed her legs in a fairly transparent attempt to look casual. Something had her rattled.

"Why would anyone want to hurt you, honey?" I asked. "It somehow doesn't feel random to me." I knew damn well it wasn't random.

"Just the price of doing business," she said as she blew a plume of smoke skyward. I still wasn't buying the casual routine.

"Donovan's trying to pin this assault on me, too, you know?"

"He's always been an asshole."

"Oh, so now you know him?"

She hesitated. "No...I...just what I've heard, just what you've told me."

Did she think I was some kind of idiot? Of course she knew him. In her line of work, it's her job to know who means what to whom. Keeping savvy was key. She knew him, all right. I should have busted her in that lie earlier.

She shifted the conversation slightly.

"This wouldn't have happened if you'd have spent the night," she said.

"Who's to say I wouldn't have been beaten up, too, honey?" I asked. "I'm a lover, not a fighter."

"Some lover," she said without trying to curb her sarcasm.

I really didn't have the time or patience for this, but I tried to keep it light. I plopped down next to her like a big kid.

"Aw, honey, you're way too much woman for me," I chided.

She turned to face me and put her hand on my knee.

"Let's both of us just split," she said, trying to sound upbeat. "We're too good for this jerkwater burgh. That is, unless you don't like me."

Her vulnerability was a little unnerving and not entirely believable. Here was a woman that usually had men wrapped around her finger so tight they were left looking like sprung springs. Now I knew she was in trouble, big trouble.

"I do like you," I said.

"You know what I mean."

"But I'm just a broke bachelor with a roving eye."

"Here, Mister Bachelor," she said, handing me a thin gift-wrapped box. "I got you a little something."

"You didn't have to..."

"Just open it."

I tore the foil wrapping paper off to reveal a box from Sibley, Lindsay & Curr. Inside, wrapped in tissue, was a blue silk necktie with a red diagonal stripe and a black diamond in the center.

"How did you know?" I asked.

"You told me you lost the other one I gave you before," she said. "Remember?"

No, actually. I didn't remember. But I'd been asking my brain to store a lot lately. Who knows what else I'd forgotten at this point.

"Well, thanks. This was very thoughtful."

"I love you," she said.

Love.

Yup, the coup de grâce, the cherry on top, the "L" word.

Love. It wasn't that I was opposed to the idea. I believed in love. Hell, I fell in love almost every day. I had pictures to prove it. I just wasn't ready to settle down. So whenever that word entered a conversation, another "L" word wasn't far behind: leaving...which I was about to get up and do when Rosa's phone rang. She ran and picked up the extension in the hallway.

I looked at the tie and scratched my head. I honestly didn't remember telling her I had lost the other one. In fact it wasn't lost, just locked away in evidence. No, I certainly wouldn't have told her that. Her half of the phone conversation derailed my train of thought.

"I told you, I haven't seen him," she said. "No...no...He should have thought of that before...Just leave me alone."

The conversation was hushed and harsh and brief. She tried to keep it quiet. She slammed the phone down ending the call with a bang.

"Bastard!" she shouted.

"Who was it?" I asked.

She quickly composed herself, lighting a cigarette with shaky hands. She snapped the lighter shut, while letting out a big cloud of smoke.

"Wrong number," she said.

Chapter 29

Though I tinkered around on my car to a certain degree, it was actually my old mechanic buddy, Mike Kelly at Kelly's West Side Sunoco Service, who did most of the work. Mike tooled around town in his flat black '32 three-window coupe in an old top hat with his wife and two bulldogs in the rumble seat. His face shared space with a snow white beard that had a mind of its own and no sense of direction, but couldn't hide his smile; he was always laughing. Those around him laughed, too, when they weren't cringing at his humor. Mike's jokes were off color and blue.

He was definitely a character whose company I thoroughly enjoyed despite his constant ribbing at my automotive jerry-rigging. Mike could fix anything, including un-screwing my screw-ups, and could make something out of nothing: air filters fashioned from old vacuum cleaner parts, valve stems capped with dice. Mike was part grease monkey, part magician, part mad scientist. He'd try and show me the right way, but ultimately wound up doing most of it himself.

My recent run-in with vandals had given him the job of fitting her with four new tires and a windshield. Not to mention fumigating the interior and giving her a general once-over. He had brought my car back to life so many times he re-named it a Mercury Lazarus. Yeah, and he was Jesus Christ with a wrench.

Mike was pounding something enthusiastically with a hammer when Mickey and I strolled in. Mike's garage was filled with cars in various stages of resuscitation and the walls were floor to ceiling with girlie pictures and outdated calendars he kept up for the nudie cuties on them. Mickey spun a 360, taking in the pin-up harem.

"Wow," he said. "Now this is a righteous hangout. I dig his decorator."

Mike looked up and grinned when he saw us—a captive audience. He hiked up his trousers and went straight into his routine.

"Well now, I ever tell you the one about the drunken sailor and the cross-eyed mermaid?" he asked.

He had, plenty of times, but I let him tell it again. It was a nice break in the action. We popped open a couple root beers out of the old Frigidaire as Mike rattled off what he'd done to my ride. New tires, new windshield, tune-up, oil change, various tweaks and adjustments, including replacing my smashed hula girl with a new and improved topless one he affectionately named *Princess Come-on-I-wanna-lay-ya.* He leaned in the passenger window and gave her a tweak, setting her off into her spring-powered hula dance.

"How about them coconuts?" he asked with a laugh. "It's gonna be hard to keep your eyes on the road."

He was right. Her constant hip swivel was hypnotic. On my way to headquarters later that night, I caught myself drifting into the oncoming lane a couple times until I finally put my hat over her. Girls of all sizes were proving to be a danger to me.

Chapter 30

Night time and HQ was a ghost town. Since I was persona non grata, this was the only time to avoid anyone in my growing fan club and get in undetected. Besides, I wasn't having a lot of luck sleeping, what with the heat and the heat that was on me.

I parked down the street and slipped in the rear entrance where the night crew would have their hands full checking in the steady parade of assorted reprobates that would continue to pour in well into sun up. No one would see me.

The place was shut down for the night with just the EXIT lights at either end left to illuminate the whole floor in a dull, darkroom red. Someone had left a fan running on their desk. It hummed weak and worthless. The whole floor was dim and dank.

There were various cork boards for open cases hanging on the walls throughout the squad room. Maps, diagrams, lists and photos all pertaining to a specific case were pinned up to be examined, re-examined, hashed, rehashed and stared at until something jumped out. This was where the detectives pow-wowed and brainstormed once all the legwork was done. This is where the pieces of the puzzle were put together.

The Vickie Hayes case was still open. A dozen or so of my shots from the crime scene were pinned up. Yet as far as I knew, nothing had jumped out to any of the detectives. Something jumped out at me: the Medical Examiner's report. The cause of death listed as cervical fracture, or in layman's terms, a broken neck. So why would the killer want to hide that fact with the necktie? My necktie?

I hit the light switch on the wall. I stood before the board and waited. I had no idea how the detectives did it. I didn't know what I was looking for, but something was gonna have to jump. I just stood there with my arms folded, frowning and squinting, awaiting a revelation.

I always shot in tight bursts, circling the victim and the overall situation, so when laying the photos out, investigators could construct a kind of 3-D diorama of the scene. Often the shots overlapped and I would get multiple takes of seemingly mundane fixtures and scenery.

One trick I'd learned in photographing models was a reversal of priorities, or more simply put, saving the best for last. In the finished picture, all eyes gravitate first to the legs, the breasts, the backside—the sweet spots, the candy, the goods. But from the photographer's perspective, if the chin isn't up, the tummy's not tucked in, the back isn't arched or the toes aren't pointed, then the shot is a wash no matter how ample the bosom, long the legs or round the derriere.

I had shot most of the Hayes crime scene on my knees, shooting across the scene at waist level of those standing in the room. Most there knew to get out of the way, but I moved fast and inevitably caught a leg or a foot here and there in the picture, or every once in awhile, a clue masquerading as something irrelevant.

So here I was in the middle of the night reversing my priorities. Forward thinking hadn't worked, why not give backwards a try?

I unfocused my eyes, relaxed and studied. I began to look at the series of photos the way I would when editing a glamour shoot. I looked at all the seemingly unimportant components in each shot first before finally arriving at the central focus, in this case, Vickie Hayes' body. I did this for close to an hour. I had just about given up and was going into a big yawn/stretch combo when something jumped, something big. I leaned in to get a better look.

It was a shot of Rossi after he had pulled back the sheet. Rossi and the body were in the foreground and Donovan stood in the back oblivious to the police work that was going on. There were four shots in rapid succession. At first glance, they were all identical, some might even argue a waste of film, but now they had paid off...big time.

In shot number one, I noticed an ashtray full of spent butts sitting on a bamboo end table. But in shot number two, the ashtray was gone. It wasn't until shot number four that it reappeared...empty. Donovan's legs were in all four shots next to the ashtray. But by shot number five, Donovan was gone, and I'm sure it was with a pocket full of cigarette butts and ashes. The question was why?

I pulled the shots off the board and laid them out on a nearby desk and flicked on its lamp. Through a magnifying glass it was clear; Donovan inching over to snag the ashtray...the ashtray full of butts, including several ultra-thin pink ones with a metallic band. Pink and gold like the cigarettes that Rosa Lee smoked. She had been there at one point, too. And for some reason Donovan didn't want anyone to know.

My brain was scrambling for some traction. I jotted a quick note. *Donovan knows something. He may even know the killer*, it said. Donovan may even be the killer, but I kept that thought to myself. *Get in touch with me ASAP.* I slipped it into an envelope along with the photos and scrawled *Det. Rossi—urgent!* on the outside. I left it at Rossi's desk, sticking out a bit in the top drawer.

Man, I needed a cold beer...or two.

Chapter 31

I made my way over to Patsy's in Kodak Park. Patsy's Pub wasn't much more than a shoebox with a good jukebox and cold beer; one of many working man's pit stops on the way home after his shift at Kodak. Patsy's was a drinking man's bar, no frills and to the point—set 'em up and knock 'em back. And of course there was Patsy Ryan with his war stories and dusty old one-liners, straight off the cob. Misery loves company but nobody cried in their beer here.

I curbed the chariot and killed the engine. The front door was propped open and half a dozen conversations ricocheted out to the sidewalk. I strolled inside.

It was like any other night at Patsy's. Kodak workers—past and present—old war vets, palookas, wisenheimers, know-it-alls, ne'er-do-wells and your run-of-the-mill bar polishers all bellied up to the bar. The Knights of the Buy-Another-Round-Table, the characters who had it all figured out, lost it and found it again somewhere towards the bottom of a glass, gin-mill wisdom, epiphanies on ice.

This wasn't a place to bring a date, or find one for that matter; Patsy's was a de facto gentlemen's club. There was no ladies room. And there was no need for excuses when wives called up because there was no phone. A man could come in here and vanish for a while.

I headed straight for the jukebox. Even when I wasn't doing anything in particular, it was nice to have a soundtrack. I fished a coupla nickels out of my jeans.

The coins clunked, the buttons thumped and the battered Wurlitzer slowly whirred to life. It was so old that it shook and rattled in protest before rolling out my selection: Big Joe Turner. You simply can't go wrong with some Big Joe Turner. While Joe gave the blues the old Kansas City shout over the jukebox's calamity, I shouted my beverage selection to Patsy.

"Hey, bartender," I said. "Pour me a Cream Ale, *por favor.*"

I sat down as the pint slid down the bar, stopping directly in front of me, its mug sweating as much as my own. Even the cigarette machine was beaded in condensation. The ceiling fan above me whooped and chopped at the thick air in vain as the jukebox's volume faded in and out. The record skipped a couple times.

"Man, Patsy," I said, "you gotta do something about that old warhorse."

"Aw, she ain't that old," Patsy said.

"Are you kidding me? When that beast rolled off the line, the Dead Sea was just sick. Hell, when it was new, dirt was still clean." I was on a roll. "When it was built, history was just called 'now.'" I left it at that; I didn't want to overdo it.

He leaned back and laughed big and loud. Everything Patsy did was big and loud. He always wore suspenders that threatened to snap at any moment, especially when he laughed. When he wasn't leaning on the bar, he towered at six-foot six and probably weighed in excess of three hundred and fifty pounds. I'd seen him bounce drunks out the front door two at a time without breaking a sweat or losing his smile. He slicked his hair back like I did and had the same devil tattoo on his forearm—purely coincidental. He got his in Hawaii during the war on a night he can't clearly recall. Mine wound up on my arm on an equally foggy night getting stewed, blued and tattooed in Brooklyn. These tattoos, along with our penchant for bad jokes, were our bond.

"What about that pothole out in front of my place you call a car?" he asked.

"It'll be finished up slick one of these days," I said. "You'll see. Besides hot rods look best a little raw, if you ask me."

"Shoot, that bucket of bolts will be lucky if it's ever a warm rod."

"Well," I said, "your daughter seems to like riding in it. Your wife, too."

The room gave off a collective "Oooh."

Advantage: Valentine.

"You fracture me, Frankie," Patsy said. "You should take that act on the road. Howsabout now?"

This is the way it would go whenever I showed up at Patsy's, a dual of digs and wisecracks with the disapproving groans of those within earshot. However, in spite of all the jokes and jabs, Patsy had a knack for putting things in perspective with a sort of bartender's intuition you just don't see much anymore. Everyone warming a stool at Patsy's Pub had something go askew at one point in his life and Patsy was keen enough to tune into it and help. Or at least offer a temporary reprieve by drowning the problem. Patsy would offer advice but never a cure; he wanted them to come back, after all. All this beer wasn't going to drink itself.

The place was beginning to thin out as those with dinner on the table went home. I was on beer number three, Etta James was on the jukebox, sobbing and shouting all sexy and cool and Patsy was on a cigarette break. He came around the bar and copped a squat next to me. His stool groaned as its legs bowed slightly.

"What's on your mind, pal?" he asked, scooting a little closer to hear over the music.

I looked around before pointing to myself.

"Who me?" I asked. "Everything's jake."

"Man, you look mighty sour for a cat who takes pictures of so much female confection. What's got you down, pal?"

"You don't wanna know," I said.

"C'mon. Whatsamatter? You fall in love again?"

"Worse."

"Try me."

"Okay." I wound up and spilled in one breath what should have taken several. "One of my models got mixed up in a blackmail scam on a pervert judge with some shady types and wound up dead. Another chick that's involved, somehow is a complete head case and is looking for love—from me. Her ex-husband—the lead detective on the case—is dirty and thinks I made it with his ex-wife—which I didn't—and is looking to hang whatever he can on me. And if that weren't enough, the father of the dead girl, who thinks I made it with his daughter—which I did—wants my head on a stake. Oh, and I'm in Dutch with the Captain. But other than that..."

Patsy just sat there rubbing his chin while I sat there waiting for some of his sage wisdom, my diatribe still hanging heavy in the humid air.

"Oh," I said, tipping my empty mug upside down, "on top of all that, my beer's gone."

He took a final drag off his cigarette and crushed it in the tin ashtray by his elbow. It had a picture of a naked girl on it and *Stolen from Patsy's* written in script along the edge with the address below, and of course, no phone number. I had a few just like it at home.

After some more chin-rubbing, he stood up with a long sigh and patted me on the back. *Aah,* I thought, *here comes the answer, the fix, the recipe, the insight, the way out, the solution.* Patsy looked at me and smiled.

"I got your tab tonight, bub," he said.

A few more beers and some more jittery jump and jive from the jukeboxasaurus and I stumbled out to my car. I had to drive; I was too loaded to walk.

Chapter 32

It was late and I was running out of options and energy. A shower would do me good. In the morning, I would go down to headquarters and talk with Rossi if he hadn't tracked me down by then. He seemed to be the only one who wasn't crooked or out to kill me. I'd show him what I'd discovered in the crime scene photos and I'd show him the pictures of the judge. I knew he'd give me a fair shake and then we could both go to Prescott. Perfect.

I flipped a U-turn and headed south. A car parked on the other side of the street pulled out behind me. I didn't pay it much mind. Lake Avenue was fairly deserted so I opened the bomb up a bit, letting the four barrels do their thing. The car behind me stayed back but kept pace. By the time I hit Maplewood Park, I was doing close to eighty and still had company. It wasn't a patrol car and it was too old to be an unmarked unit. It had to be Eddie Hayes. I sobered up pronto.

As we approached downtown, traffic began to pick up, but I kept up the speed in hopes a cop might take notice and intercede. No such luck tonight.

I would've rolled the red light by the button factory in High Falls, but there were too many cars. I stopped. Hayes didn't and slammed into the back of me. The impact pitched me forward and I smacked my head on the steering wheel. By the time I came to, I was being yanked out of the car. Hayes was nowhere in sight.

"Hey," I said. "What gives?"

The two rather large collegiate types said nothing. They had me pinned up against my car. One hit me in the stomach and all the wind left me. I started to go down. Fortunately, the following upper cut kept me from hitting the ground. For a moment I was weightless before gravity returned. I staggered back, holding my jaw. I could taste blood. I was sure happy it wasn't Hayes, but was puzzled as to who these two jokers were.

"Stay away from Nancy, Valentine," one of them said. I racked my throbbing brain as air slowly squeaked back into my lungs. I spit on the ground. It was beginning to make sense.

Models who were willing—and qualified—to add some va-va to the voom, a little ooh to the la la weren't in big supply. Most of them were just fun time party girls or co-eds working their way through school. And it always seemed the most flirtatious and rambunctious chicks—the kind I liked—gravitated to blockheads like these—enormous, ex-jock, he-man gorillas fueled by jealousy and violence. Blue pics can cost a fella black eyes.

"Nancy...Nancy," I said. "Oh, Nancy. Nice rack, washed up football player with a pencil dick for a boyfriend. Yeah, Nancy, I've been meaning to call her. I think she left some underwear at my pad. How's she doing, anyway?"

I didn't wait for a response and punched the one who hadn't said anything dead in the nose. It made a sickening crunch. He howled as blood immediately began to gush. I wound up for number two when the other one kicked my legs out from under me and I hit the pavement. I scrambled and tried to slide under the car and got almost all the way under it before they both dragged me back. This was going to be bad. I balled up as best I could, just waiting for the tap dance to begin.

It never did.

The clearing of a throat and the audible click of a bullet being chambered brought the curtain down on the bullies' ballet before it began. I uncovered my head and looked up to see Nancy's gorilla with the muzzle of a .45 auto pressed to his cheek, mashing his face into an awkward kiss. He was completely frozen. He had pissed himself.

The man with the gun spoke in a voice so husky it could've pulled a dogsled.

"Apologize to the man," he said, jamming the gun harder up against the kid's cheek. The kid looked sideways at the gun, his eyes as big as fried eggs. He held his hands out palms down as if to smooth out the situation.

"T-take it easy, man," fried eggs said. "This is just a simple misunderstanding. Christ, don't shoot!"

The big voice spoke again, louder.

"Apologize."

They both stammered a panicked apology in unison and set to running when my Samaritan fired the .45 into the air.

"Thanks, pal," I said, reaching out my hand for some help up. He ignored it. I struggled to my feet slow and solo.

"The judge wants to see you," he said. Man, he looked familiar. It took me a minute before the light bulb went on. It was my old pal Sasquatch, the same goon who was with Donovan during our little kibitz in the confessional.

"What Judge?" I asked as I brushed myself off.

"Don't get cute."

He motioned towards his car.

"Get in," he said.

Despite his gracious offer, I wanted to keep my options open and my body above ground. This guy worked for the judge and with Donovan, things were definitely not on the level. And he carried a gun, a big gun.

"Gee, thanks," I said. "But if it's all the same to you, I'll follow."

"Park it, wise guy. You're riding with me."

I pulled my car into a spot along the curb. I could've gunned it and left him in the dust, but now curiosity was gnawing at me. In a weird way I was actually looking forward to meeting his honor. Besides, I was too tired to fight anymore.

He cordially opened the back door of a late model garbage bin on wheels. It looked lived in. There was a musty blanket bunched up on the back seat with what appeared to be dried blood on it and old newspapers strewn about. There was a large shovel as well. The whole vehicle was a rolling crime scene. On the floor was a soft leather briefcase. I looked at it while trying not to look like I was looking at it—which is harder than it sounds. It was embossed with initials MFC by the handle. I played them over and over in my head. MFC, MFC, MFC...Michael Francis Conway. I wasn't so curious anymore.

We pulled out with a loud squeal and headed north on Lake Avenue down to Ridge Road and hung a right.

"Where're we going?" I asked. I didn't expect an answer. I didn't get one. I just looked out the window as my life rapidly passed me by.

Chapter 33

A gravel driveway snaked its way up an immaculate hill of lilac bushes to an imposing and elaborate wrought iron gate at the top. The scripted initials were so swirly and ornate that they were virtually illegible. I was pretty sure I could make out a *J*.

"We're here," Sasquatch said into the intercom at the gate. The little speaker barked something back and the gate slowly swung open to reveal yet even more driveway leading to a large English Tudor job covered by a century of ivy.

Two Dobermans announced our arrival loudly. They came bounding out to the car and pounced on it, snarling and slobbering on the windows. Their sleek physiques and bared fangs indicated a deep-seated anger fueled by hunger; their owner kept them hungry for a reason. They eyeballed me like steak through the car window. I didn't feel all that delicious and just sat in the car until one of the three garage doors went up. A shrill whistle from within cut the air and Rommel and Panzer retreated to their posts.

Out strolled the Honorable Judge Preston Jenkins, the source of the whistle and the man in the photos. He wore white linen trousers and a cream-colored leisure cut shirt that showed off his tan. His hair was wavy and pure silver. He looked like a diplomat as he walked towards us with a confident swagger full of elegance and a dash of arrogance. He flashed me a big grin and took my hand before I could offer it. I knew of him vaguely through the papers and whatnot. And thanks to this whole picture caper, I now knew him even more than he probably wanted. More than I really needed to know any man, frankly. People saw him as upstanding and moral, an all-around square American. I knew he'd be angling for the evidence that would indicate otherwise. If it got out, it would ruin him.

As a candidate, Jenkins' campaign promise was tough on crime, big on family. His wife and two sons made frequent appearances with him as he mugged and waved his way to the top. The last election for family court judge had been a landslide in Jenkins' favor. With a mixture of savvy, charisma and rakish good looks—and his opponent caught *in flagrante delicto* in a linen closet with a cocktail waitress, at one of his own fundraisers, no less—Jenkins cruised to victory.

He occupied various committees, sat on assorted boards of directors, was a member of The County Club, The Yacht Club, The Gun Club and a handful of charitable organizations. Jenkins had a lot of weight and money to throw around. They named buildings and streets after guys like this.

"Mister Valentine," he said. "Big fan, big fan of your work."

"Yeah?" I asked, sounding fairly nonplussed.

"I love your taste in women. Where do you find these exquisite creatures?"

"Living or dead?" I asked.

Sasquatch smacked me in the back of my head. I almost choked on my gum.

"Which way you wanna wind up, smart mouth?" he asked. "Huh? It's up to you."

Jenkins put up his hand.

"Relax, Lenny, Mister Valentine is our guest." He turned and smiled a broad display of perfect teeth. "Won't you join me for a drink?"

"Hell," I said, "it's your party."

He was cordial and treated me as if I were a guest, free to come and go as I pleased. However, with Lenny now playing the part of my shadow, I knew otherwise.

We went in through the garage up the back stairs to a spacious lounge overlooking the large in-ground pool. It had a "men only" feel to it, all wood and leather. I got the impression Mrs. Jenkins had never been here. It smelled of cigars and money. A large pool table with red felt occupied the center of the room. One wall was floor to ceiling with books and the remaining walls were occupied by numerous heads of animals that, while still attached to their bodies, had once roamed freely about the Serengeti or the American Southwest before the arrival of Jenkins and a .30-06. Nude paintings on black velvet—notably a gorgeous Polynesian princess by Edgar Leeteg—and nude figure studies and photographs, including one of my earlier endeavors, punctuated the blank stares of the glass-eyed taxidermy. It was of a young Mexican girl posing with a pink satin pillow on black velvet wearing nothing more than opera gloves and a smile, her beautiful backside hoisted suggestively in the air. I think her name was Anna.

Lenny stood by the door, his arms folded. Jenkins walked over to the bar. I spoke up.

"Man, what a rumpus room," I said. "I dig the artwork."

"I told you I was a fan," he said, motioning to the picture. "That's one of my favorites."

"I'm glad you dig it, your honor," I said. "But you and I both know that's not why I'm here. What do you want?"

"I admire your candor, Mister Valentine," he said, while pouring himself a drink. "I'll get to the point. I'm a fan of Mickey Miller's work as well. Are you familiar with him?"

"Mickey? Yeah, I know him," I said.

Jenkins got more to the point.

"From what I understand, you have some of his work, too. Work that belongs to me."

"I'm not sure I know what you're talking about."

Lenny gave me a kidney punch and I dropped to one knee. I started to push myself to my feet and he stepped on my hand. I let out a yell. Jenkins didn't stop him this time; he leaned down and continued to smile that winning smile.

"No more games," he said. "I need those pictures now, Mister Valentine. Now. Do I make myself clear?"

I was fairly certain he wouldn't kill me as long as I had what he wanted, but he could certainly put on the hurt. So naturally, I made with the funny routine.

"C'mon Jenkins," I said. "People will understand. Besides, you've got great legs." I had enough air back in me to let out a low wolf whistle. "Those are some stems, daddy-o. What a fine pair of getaway sticks you have, your honor. And talk about rough trade..."

Lenny seemed confused.

"What's he talking about?" he asked. I didn't imagine Jenkins would've told him. Jenkins was in a position that demanded respect, respect from constituents, respect from voters and respect from subordinates. Guys like Lenny were told what to do, when to do it, where to do it and who to do it to, but rarely, if ever, why. The public was told who to like, and they generally went along until it crossed the line into weird territory.

People were willing to forgive a momentary indiscretion every now and then from their public servants; they were only human, after all. Hell, at this point it was practically expected. Folks had seen enough exposés of public leaders dishing out moist-eyed *mea culpas* while the dutiful wife stood by her man. By now it had become rather routine.

Even damning evidence like a set of pictures of said fallen leader in the throes of indiscrete passion would ultimately get dismissed after a little eye-bugging and tongue-wagging. But a lot of the male population was in no position to point fingers. It was that whole people in glass houses thing. Consequently, political scandals like this burned out quickly.

However, when the public figure in question had gone the deviant route like this, people were gonna talk. And cavemen like Lenny here simply would not understand. Jenkins was a cross-dressing tart, a transvestite, a queen. And his majesty certainly didn't want to be crowned in public. Even his royal bodyguard was in the dark.

And of course every court needs a jester.

I looked up at Lenny and started to laugh.

"You don't know?" I asked."Your boss here is a Cinderella fella, a real glamour gir..."

Jenkins kicked me in the side of the head so hard it felt like it spun completely around. I was out before I hit the floor, my record now o and three.

Chapter 34

It was so pitch black when I came to that I wasn't sure if I'd actually come to. But the throbbing in my head told me I was awake and officially in too deep. I was on my side. My hands were tied behind me. My feet were tied, too. When I tried to straighten up, the gag in my mouth prevented a painful yelp that would have rivaled Tarzan's from leaving my throat.

My eyes began to adjust with the help of a sliver of light coming from under the door. I was in a bedroom lying on the floor at the foot of the bed. I managed to sit up despite the dozen or so monkeys dosed on Benzedrine playing bongos in my skull. I could make out a reflection in the dressing table mirror—hoping it wasn't mine. The poor slob looked tore up from the floor up. Between him and I were various women's amenities: a can of hairspray, some ornate bottles of perfume, several faceless mannequin heads–one wearing a vaguely familiar blonde wig–and assorted hair care accessories, including some scissors. I began to scoot towards them, stopping when I could hear voices. Lenny was talking.

"Pictures of you and some broad," he was saying. "So what? You're a ladies man. People will understand. You're going to an awful lot of trouble. What's all the panic?"

The hospitality and civility were gone from Jenkins' voice. He copped an icy tone.

"Look," he said, "I don't pay you to ask questions. Your pal Conway asked questions and that's why he's playing a harp."

The judge continued, his voice grave and determined. "This Valentine character has those pictures, I just know it," he said. "We'll keep him on ice until he gives them up or until we track them down. I've got Donovan on it now."

Lenny grunted in the affirmative.

I slid over to the wall next to the dressing table and pushed myself up. My ears began to ring in time to the conga-beating skull monkeys and I came from within an inch of passing out. I sat on the edge of the bed until the spinning stopped. I was soaked in sweat.

Loud, heavy footsteps in double time announced the arrival of someone else in the other room. I strained to hear what was happening.

"I got 'em, I got 'em," the new arrival said. "Son of a bitch thought he was slick hiding them in the wheel well."

It was Donovan. He had found the pictures. I got up, spun around, grabbed the scissors and began to saw at the rope around my wrists. They'd be coming in any minute now to give me the big *adios* and I didn't wanna be here when they did. I hate goodbyes.

"Nice work, Lloyd," the judge said. "I'll just put...hey, what do you think you're doing?"

"Not so fast," Donovan said. "Why don't I hold onto these for you, your honor? They might come in handy down the road. That is, unless you have your checkbook handy."

"Put that away, you fool," Jenkins shouted.

Lenny piped in.

"Drop it," he said to Donovan.

Donovan laughed. "You wouldn't shoot a cop would you?" he asked Lenny. Donovan's bluff turned out to be

Donovan's blunder. There was a short scuffle. Two loud pops cut the air, followed by a heavy thud. Then it was quiet. Jenkins finally spoke up.

"I never trusted that fat bastard," he said. "Get him out of here. We've got to get moving. That degenerate Miller will no doubt have copies...that Lee broad, too. We've got to shut them up for good. I'm not taking any chances."

"What about Valentine?" Lenny asked.

"Right. Take care of that, too."

That was my cue. I heard it loud and clear and really started hacking away at my bonds. Time was running out.

Jenkins got on the phone. He cleared his throat and lowered his voice an octave.

"Hello, Rosa," he said in a honeyed tone. "Yes, hello, my darling..."

I couldn't hear anything else over the thumping and scuffling and dragging—Donovan's corpulent carcass no doubt. Donovan was a dirty cop. And now he was dead.

As far as I could figure, Vickie and Mickey had picked the wrong man to blackmail. They had poked a rattlesnake, a connected rattlesnake, a connected rattlesnake that could kill a cop as easily as have him on the payroll. Me, Mickey and Rosa were the remaining loose ends Lenny had to tighten up for the judge...starting with me.

I got the ropes cut in what seemed like forever and made it to the window that looked over the back end of a golf course. I flipped the latch but ivy had grown thick all throughout the window frame. It wouldn't budge. The sound of smashing glass would tip Lenny off to my departure. I would only have one chance to split.

I pulled off the bedspread and mummified my arm. I made a fist, wound up and punched out the entire window with three decisive jabs. I pulled myself out the window, climbed down the twisted ivy and was running before my feet even hit the ground. The grass was damp and the bedspread around my arm got snagged in the jagged glass along the windowsill. I started to slip but it stopped me short and spun me back around just in time to see Lenny hoisting himself out the window, his gun drawn. I virtually twisted my arm out of its socket to get free and was halfway down the hill when the first of several shots rang out, followed by the angry scream of bullets. They whizzed by so close I could feel their heat. Lenny was out the window and barreling toward me. I could hear barking in the distance. It was getting closer. I turned around in time to see Jenkins' hounds tackle Lenny, one hitting him high, the other low. He let out a scream as the dogs tore into him. I poured on the steam as a burst of gunfire went off behind me. The barking ceased.

I ran and ran until I was well into the woods. I ducked down behind a tree to catch my breath before cautiously looking back toward the house. The coast was clear.

Chapter 35

My whole body ached as I made it to the road. I was spent and running purely on fear dipped in adrenaline. I trudged about two miles, ducking into the brush with each passing car until I came to a filling station. It was locked up for the evening but had a working pay phone next to a self-help air compressor. I fumbled in my pocket for a dime and dropped it in. Mickey's number just rang and rang. Naturally. However, Rosa picked up eventually. I cut her hello in half.

"Get out of the house now," I said hoarsely and still out of breath. My chest and head were one big thundering heartbeat.

"I'm expecting company," she said. "What's wrong? Where are you? What's going on?"

"That company is going to kill you," I said. "Get out of the house and come pick me up. It's all coming down now."

She hesitated.

"But I just..."

I was frantic.

"Get out of there now, goddammit!" I yelled.

I stood out of sight in the shadows along the side of the filling station and waited for my ride.

As far as Jenkins was concerned, I was in the wind and didn't have the photos. But I suspected Mickey had copies of the photos and Rosa might as well. But the judge and Lenny weren't going to ask nicely.

Rosa's roadster flew into the driveway at lightning

speed, then back out again, with me half in, half out, trying to close the passenger door.

If Mickey were hip to what was going down he would've already taken a powder by now. But if he hadn't, I was pretty sure he'd be trolling his usual Friday night haunt. If he had copies of the pictures, I could get them to Rossi or even Prescott. If he didn't, I was screwed. Regardless, Jenkins and Lenny would be looking for him, and it wasn't going to end pretty.

Rosa wore a pair of tight denim pedal-pushers that made her legs twice as long and a red and white gingham blouse with nothing underneath.

She caught me looking.

"You like?" she asked playfully.

"Honey, can't you see I'm a little distracted right now?" I asked. "Just head to The Embassy, please."

Rosa cracked a cockeyed grin.

"You know," she said, "they think you killed her."

I wasn't sure I heard her right.

"What?"

"If you'd been with me last night, I could've been your alibi. I could still be your alibi if you like..."

I didn't follow.

"Last night?" I asked. "What the hell are you talking about? What the hell's last night got to do with it? Vickie's been dead for almost..."

"Gail," she said with an odd smirk. "Gail Donovan. I'm talking about Gail Donovan."

"What about Gail?" I asked in alarm. The last thing I needed was these two dizzy dames joining forces.

"She was found dead in her apartment early this morning. Her neck was broken just like Vickie's. The cops are looking for you, Frankie." She seemed to take some pleasure in announcing all of this to me.

"Gail's dead?" I asked. "What the...?"

"I know you didn't kill anybody, honey," she said.

"You're goddamned right I didn't," I said. "Judge Jenkins did."

Rosa looked a little surprised.

"Jenkins," she said.

"What's Jenkins to you?" I asked.

"Just a friend," she said.

"A friend who wants you dead, you know? He killed Vickie, he killed Gail, he killed Donovan and two private dicks. The bodies are piling up. Nothing's gonna stop this guy. He's after you and Mickey now...and me!"

"Nobody's gonna hurt you," she said with the same smirk.

"What's so funny?" I asked. "He wants to fit us all for wooden kimonos. What is wrong with you?"

She said nothing and started to laugh. It spread. What else could I do? I started to laugh, laugh at my current situation, laugh at the danger I was in, just laugh and laugh and laugh until tears streamed down my face. I was a punch line without a joke.

Neighbors had seen me walk into Gail's building. They mistook the carnal calamity for violence and now she was dead. I couldn't figure how she tied in. Donovan had just discovered the pictures before getting greedy and then getting dead. Perhaps he thought I stashed them with her. Jenkins had to know Gail Donovan had nothing to do with her ex-husband. But maybe he was desperate enough to get all existing copies of the pictures and was indiscriminately punching tickets. He wasn't going to rule anyone out. I hoped to hell Mickey had lied to me; chances were he had. The man was too much of a quick-buck opportunist to not have some copies squirreled away.

Jenkins had sent Lenny over to shake Rosa up and

get the pictures from her the day before. She didn't have them, or didn't let on she did. But she could still talk. And that was a chance Jenkins probably didn't want to take.

Chapter 36

We sped down a one-way off Main and cut into the alley behind The Embassy. It was break time between shows and the boys in the band and some of the girls–some wearing nothing more than their dressing gowns–were talking, smoking, laughing, goofing around by the stage door. A dice game had started up along the wall. I jumped out and broke up the party.

"Anybody seen Mickey?" I asked, out of breath as if I'd run the whole way there.

"Mickey?" asked a very petite redhead in a very petite robe that was doing a lousy job covering her not-so-petite artillery. She had a Sunday school face with a body that said Saturday night. She slinked toward me in sling-back heels like I was prey. She leaned in close. "You know him?"

"Sure," I said, momentarily distracted.

"Tell him to give Sugar a call, would ya?"

She and the girls she had been standing with burst into giggles with wiggles to match. All the girls wanted Mickey. All the guys wanted to be Mickey, but not tonight they didn't. One of the cats rolling bones spoke up.

"He spends weekends shooting down at that motor lodge just south of Watkins Glen," he said. "Nice waterfalls, cabins, the works. It's a bit of a haul, but you might wanna check down there."

Ernie came out of the backstage door lighting a cigarillo. His face was covered in lipstick and his shirt was tucked half in, half out. He shook out the match and walked over to the car.

"Nice ride," he said, sniggering. "Where'd you ever...what the hell happened to you?" I ignored his question.

"I gotta find Mickey now," I said.

Ernie looked puzzled.

"Funny," he said, combing his hair back with his fingers. "But you're the second one tonight looking for Mick. He in some kinda trouble?"

"Who's been asking?" I asked anxiously.

"Don't know if they were cops," he said. "But their car had official plates of some kind." He pointed toward the end of the alley where I'd pulled in.

"Gosh. They was just here."

I shoved Rosa over into the shotgun seat so hard with my hip that she bounced up against the passenger door.

"Hey," she protested.

I dropped it into reverse and stood on the gas, kicking up gravel, fishtailing and squealing out of the alley as Ernie waved. Chalet Leon was just a little over ninety miles away.

Chapter 37

Chalet Leon was an old motor lodge along Route 414 with about a dozen rustic little cabins nestled next to Hector Falls. The falls spilled down one hundred sixty-five feet into Seneca Lake below. According to Indian folklore, this is where God put his hand on the region, resulting in the five Finger Lakes. Vineyards and wineries lined the winding roads throughout the region. From the Chalet's property, you could see the entire lake. It was breathtaking. I would plop a deck chair right in the stream that splashed and swirled down from the upper level into the falls themselves. I'd just sit there for hours contemplating my belly button until the sun went down to the rushing water's symphonic roar. I always came down here when I could to shoot models in and around the falls or to simply get away for a few days. I didn't tell a lot of folks about this place; I didn't want it getting overrun with tourists, their kids, pets and cookouts. This was my Shangri-la. Mine. I did tell Mickey, though.

Liz Grant had run the place for years after hanging up her clippers. Liz used to have a barbershop on South Clinton for years, where besides scoring a mean high and tight, balboa or flattop, you could meet all sorts of characters who congregated there. This was where you got the gossip; this was where you got the low-down and the news. Liz came out to the Chalet with her now-deceased husband for a long time. When the old lady who had owned the place since before the war retired, Liz jumped at the opportunity to step in and run it.

Liz's sidekick was an imposing husky-shepherd mix named Beau. Beau was a watchdog that didn't discriminate. He was thorough; he bit everybody.

Chapter 38

Jenkins and Lenny had a head start and Mickey had no clue. The clock was ticking, but I needed to make a quick stop before jetting out to the motel. Besides, a phone call would be quicker.

We swung by Carl's on my way to the expressway. A little insurance felt like a good idea about now. Rosa stayed behind in the car, filing her nails. Something was going on with her; the world was on fire around her yet she was being entirely too cool. It was a bit unsettling.

Carl lived on the second floor above the store. I sprinted to the door and rang the buzzer. I leaned on the button until the upstairs light came on. Carl opened the door in his robe, one hand thrust in his pocket. He kept it there until he saw it was me. Good news or good people with good intentions usually didn't drop by this late at night.

"I need a piece," I said flatly.

He raised his eyebrows at my attempt at gun-savvy slang. I guess it sounded a bit forced. I rephrased.

"I need to borrow a gun," I said. "C'mon, I'm in a hurry." He folded his arms and just stared back at me. I could see the advice, the warning, the refusal forming on his face. I didn't give it a chance to solidify.

"No time to explain, Carl," I said. The way he refolded his arms and shifted his weight to the other foot told me I'd have to try anyway. I was still breathing hard. Between breaths, the words came out garbled, backwards and sounding somewhat insane.

He didn't let me finish and simply motioned me to follow him.

"I hope you know what you're doing," he said as he unlocked the iron grate in front of the store. It squeaked loudly as he rolled it back.

"Of course, I don't know what I'm doing," I said. "I know what I should've done and what needs to be done now otherwise more people are gonna wind up dead."

"Including you, smart guy," he said as I followed him to the back of his shop.

"That's what I'm trying to avoid," I said. "Let me use your phone, will ya?"

As he was jingling his keys, unlocking a large cabinet, I got on the phone to ring up the Chalet. It just rang and rang and rang.

"C'mon, c'mon," I said as I stomped my foot. I was just about to slam down the receiver when Liz finally picked up on her end.

"Beau!" she shouted at her barking dog before adopting her creamy and cordial motel proprietress tone. "Good evening, Chalet Leon."

I let out a barrage of words like a Gatling gun, but managed to include most of the important details I needed, especially "Was Mickey there?" and "Had anyone else called?" She answered yes to both.

"Mickey's been here since this afternoon," she said. "And a couple of his friends called about an hour ago, said they wanted to surprise him."

The Chalet was a little over an hour away. They'd be there soon.

"Liz, those guys are bad news," I said. "You gotta hold them off. Stall them if you can until I get there. Better yet, call the State Police."

"What should I tell them?" She was beginning to sound alarmed.

"Tell them something bad is about to go down. And you better warn Mickey to hightail it out of there."

"Okay," she said. "Let me just take care of...hey! What are you doing?"

I heard the phone drop and the sounds of a scuffle before it all got drowned out by Beau's vicious bark.

"Liz...Liz!" I yelled into the phone. The line went dead.

I slammed down the receiver before dialing in to the dispatch desk. I gave Alice the Chalet's address and told her to roust Detective Rossi wherever he was.

"Tell him it's urgent," I said. "I know who killed Vickie Hayes and Gail Donovan," I said. "And it ain't me. Tell him to hurry."

Chapter 39

I hung up the phone and leaned on the counter to collect my thoughts and my breath. I now had a pulse in my stomach. I was coiled tight. I heaved a sigh and stretched my neck back and forth. It made several loud and rather unnatural cracks. Upon my third twist and pop, I glanced into Robert's work area. The walls were covered with girlie pictures, covered with girlie pictures I had taken over the years...covered with girlie pictures I had just taken. I stopped my chiropractic cha-cha and walked toward the makeshift gallery full of the long-limbed, lusty, busty and beautiful...and the odd.

I've always been an open-minded cat. You can live and let live in whatever clothes you want in my book. But there's always been something about drag queens that gets me. You simply can't tone down a man's angular harshness—the Adam's apple, the nose, the five o'clock shadow, the hip-less swivel and heavy swagger. And if you put that next to a bodacious bombshell like Vickie Hayes, I don't care how handsome you are, you're a gargoyle, you're just plain ugly and the jig is up. The pictures on the wall of Vickie and the judge proved my point and gave me a shudder. Good ol' Robert's tastes were getting more sophisticated. He had made himself some copies.

I tore them off the wall and shoved them into an envelope.

"Tell Robert I'll get these back to him," I said to Carl as he handed me an old German Luger and a sock full of bullets. He showed me how to load it and I stuck it in my waistband. I started to thank him, but he cut me off with a wave of his hand. I turned and trotted toward the car as he called out behind me.

"Be careful," he said. "That thing hasn't been fired since the war."

Chapter 40

I let the Hemi roar as the 250 horses under the Jaguar's hood had it flying east down the highway. The speedometer went up to one hundred and twenty, but I had the needle buried past it. My Merc would have blown up just thinking about it. Even with the hammer down, this baby just purred. Unfortunately, I was in no mood to marvel at the expert engineering.

The moon gave the landscape a buttery glow beneath a blanket of stars. The romance was lost on me. Not on Rosa, though. She sat next to me smiling. If the wind hadn't been roaring in my ears, I would've sworn she was humming something. She seemed happy. It was beginning to make me angry. She looked at me and smiled sweetly. That was it; I couldn't contain myself any longer.

"What the hell are you smiling about?" I asked.

She reached over and gave me a playful jab.

"I'm just happy to be here with you." She slid over closer and breathed hot in my ear. Her hair whipped about our faces and I had to push her aside to see. Her hand was on my thigh. Her blouse was open and she was spilling out. She was pulling out all the tricks. Ordinarily I'm not the type of guy who puts on the brakes when a gal is on the make.

"Don't you realize what's going on?" I asked. "We're in hot water. There're people who want me dead, in jail or both. And because of me, you're mixed up in this, too." It had also crossed my mind that because of *her*, I had gotten mixed up in this, but it seemed pointless.

"It'll all work out," she said.

Up ahead a flatbed with crates of vegetables was taking its time. I laid on the horn, but he just kept on puttering. Out of time and patience, I gunned the motor and crossed the center line coming face to face with a pair of headlights bearing down on us. A quick cut to the right and I made the tight squeeze back into the right lane as if I were threading a needle. The truck driver was forced to brake hard and let out with an angry blast from his horn. This failed to rattle Rosa all that much.

"Slow down, honey," she said. "We'll get there soon enough."

She went back to humming her inaudible tune. This chick was out of her mind, more so than most.

Chapter 41

We pulled into the lot and I jammed the car right behind a dark green Cadillac with official plates.

"Goddammit," I said. "They're already here."

I told Rosa to wait in the car and ran into the lobby. The lights were out. I felt around on the wall until I found the switch. The place was a wreck. Keys were scattered all over the counter and there was blood spattered on the carpet. It didn't look good.

A muffled groan came from the back room. I hastily tossed aside some chairs blocking the doorway to find Liz on the floor, blood coming from a cut on her head. She tried to sit up. Beau was next to her, licking his hind quarters. It looked like he'd been shot. I helped Liz up to a sitting position.

"Two goons," she said. "They're in cabin number seven with Mickey."

I ran out to the car to get Rosa and all her sing-songy sunshine madness.

"Look," I said, "I need your help."

"Anything you want, Frankie," she said. "Anything." She followed me back inside.

"Get on the phone and call an ambulance for Liz and stay here." Beau limped out as I headed towards the door. It looked like he had only been grazed, but he was clearly distressed that his master was hurt. He got between me and the exit so I bent down to console him.

"Who's a good boy?" I asked.

He bit me.

The cabins were all arranged around large maple and

pine trees along a well worn path of gravel and busted flagstone which led haphazardly to the waterfalls. It was jagged and uneven and looked like it had been fed a steady diet of twisted ankles and skinned knees over the years. The moon was higher now, illuminating my way somewhat. I didn't have time to wait for my eyes to adjust, so I made my way as quickly and carefully as I could, the Luger held out in front of me. Mickey had rented cabin number seven at the very end, right next to the falls.

I snuck along the back of the cabins until I got to number seven. The roar of the falls grew louder as I got closer, yet the sound of voices clashing in a heated argument cut through. I crept up and peered in the open window to see Mickey propped up in a chair.

He was slouched a bit and his face was a mess. Blood was running down his undershirt and he seemed to be fading in and out of consciousness. Two young women dolled up in lingerie were huddled together against the wall in quiet hysterics. Their photo shoot had been cut short. The Honorable Judge Jenkins had taken up a spot in a chair by the door. He sat with his legs crossed as he coolly oversaw the proceedings.

Lenny pulled out a large switchblade and held it next to Mickey's ear. Lenny sneered and got in Mickey's face. He was enjoying this. Mickey wasn't, but was still able to crack wise. He and I both suffered from this affliction.

"What, are you gonna kiss me, sweetheart?" he asked, making with a couple of smooching sounds. "You're really not my type."

"Gonna be pretty hard to take pictures with no eyes, asshole," Lenny shot back. "So I'm gonna ask you one more time; where are those goddamn photographs?"

"I'm tellin' ya, I ain't got any pictures," Mickey shouted, squirming away from the blade. He spit blood defiantly on the floor. Mickey wasn't leaving the judge too many options and his time was running out.

Other than some skeet shooting I had done as a boy at Rochester Brooks Gun Club with my dad, I had never really been around guns. And I had never fired a pistol before. Here I was anyway and it was now or never. How hard could it be? I made my move and raised the Luger. I pointed at the center of Lenny's broad back, squeezed the trigger and hit Mickey in the shoulder. I heard him let out a scream as the recoil from the shot knocked me off balance and off my feet. Before I could stand up, a deafening torrent of bullets came flying out of the window with bits of wood, glass and curtain. I scrambled to my feet and dove into the bushes.

My ears were ringing loudly from the Luger's antique blast. I could hear the girls screaming. I could hear Mickey moaning and I could hear the judge hollering for them to all shut up. His voice cracked. He was beginning to lose his cool. Lenny came running out of the cabin, heading toward the path he must have assumed I'd taken. He was right, dead right. As he charged straight for the thicket I was crouched behind, I took aim at the middle of his chest, squinting in anticipation of the gun's thunder and kick. I began to squeeze the trigger.

Two shots rang out and Lenny jerked up and back, falling dead two feet in front of me, a hole in the middle of his forehead, the back of his head gone. I hadn't shot him. I never got off a shot. I looked down at the gun. I looked down at Lenny's body. It was twitching and his brains looked like they were crawling out of his skull. I fought the urge to get sick and barely won. There was a heavy hand on my shoulder. I looked up. It was Eddie Hayes.

"Christ, I'm dead," I said.

"C'mon, you," he said, hoisting me up by my arm. He looked down at the Luger still in my hand and let out a disgusted laugh.

"What do you think you're going to do with that?" he asked.

Leaning down, he picked up Lenny's .45, chambered a bullet and handed it to me.

"C'mon. You're my back-up."

We ran back for the cabin where I found the judge grappling with Mickey.

"Hold it," Hayes shouted. "Nobody move." They both stopped and looked up as he leveled his gun at the judge. Jenkins' eyes darted about the room for options or perhaps allies. He found none.

"It's over, Jenkins," Hayes said, motioning to the chair by the door. "Sit."

Hayes turned to me. He kept his gun on the judge.

"Angelo says you know the score," he said to me. "That you know who killed my little girl."

Mickey was propped up against the bed with the two models attending to his wounds. This cat was simply unbelievable; even in the midst of this bedlam, Mickey had a gorgeous bird on each arm.

Court was in session and I was presiding. Hayes had commandeered the proceedings and had given me the floor.

I started in on the judge, stalling a little for time, wondering when the cops would arrive. Not that I cared, but I was fairly certain Hayes was gonna kill Jenkins as soon as he found out. My safety wasn't guaranteed either; Eddie Hayes and I had only been friends for less than five minutes.

"Folks will see these pictures and you're going to go down as the Nancy-boy freak you are," I said. "The cops will connect the dots and you'll take the rap for five murders. I can see the headlines now: JUDGE JENKINS: FROM THE BENCH TO THE CHAIR."

He looked at me arrogantly, defiantly, but toned down the attitude when his eyes fell on the gun still in my white-knuckled hand.

"Five murders?" he asked. "What five murders? You don't know what you're talking about."

"Don't play stupid with me." I raised the gun slightly and tightened my grip.

"Take it easy, V-Valentine," he said, slowly realizing the seriousness of the situation.

He just looked at me. I could hear Hayes breathing loud and hard through his nose like a leaky radiator. I continued.

"Vickie Hayes, Donovan, Donovan's wife, Mike Conway the snoop you hired to squash this in the first place, and his partner," I said. "Donovan was dirty, granted. And so was Conway. Nobody will miss either one of them. Vickie had you on the blackmail angle, but I still don't understand why you killed Gail."

Jenkins returned to higher ground and just smirked at me. I started to get hot, the gun in my hand gave me guts despite my frayed nerves. I moved in closer to him. He couldn't read me. He was visibly nervous.

"I don't know what you're talking about," he said.

Hayes lunged forward and punched the judge squarely in the face. It made a loud crack. The momentum upended his chair and he went somersaulting backwards into the wall.

Hayes stood over Jenkins with his foot on his throat, hissing through his teeth. Jenkins struggled and gurgled. Hayes pointed his gun at Jenkins' face and pulled the hammer back. It was all coming to a boil.

"The cops are on their way," I said, hoping I was right. Hayes didn't budge.

I could see the fear flush on the judge's face. So could Hayes; he was savoring it.

Jenkins' eyes began to dart back and forth. He licked his lips. He swallowed hard.

"Blackmail? Th-there was no blackmail," he stammered.

Mickey chimed in.

"See? I told you," he said. He was holding a towel to his shoulder. "And now someone hauls off and shoots me? This beats all. I'm a victim of circumstance here."

"Yeah, I'm sorry about that," I said. "I was aiming for the gorilla who was about to fit you for an eye patch."

"Christ, you shot me, Frank. What's the matter with you?"

"You still got both your eyeballs, right?"

"Shut up!" Hayes hollered.

Jenkins' version of the truth resumed.

"Mister Conway turned out to be in business for himself, so he was let go."

"Yeah, let go off a bridge," I said. Jenkins ignored me.

"So I sent Donovan over there to retrieve any duplicates of the pictures after I got word Vickie had been murdered. I didn't need them surfacing during any kind of investigation. I had nothing to do with her death. I liked her." He looked over at me. "I mean, c'mon, you've seen her. She was a good time."

Just what a good time's Dad wants to hear.

Hayes heard this and stood a little harder on Jenkins' neck. The judge was gasping for air but kept on talking.

"And Donovan," he said. "Lenny shot Donovan and killed Conway. And like you said, they were dirty. Who'll miss the bums?"

"And what about his ex?" I asked. "What about Gail Donovan?"

"I had nothing to..."

"I killed her," Rosa said. She was standing in the doorway behind me holding the envelope of pictures and a gun. Her forearm was ragged and bloody; it looked like a dog bite.

She smiled at me. Not a pretty smile, but one of those freshly cracked, detached smiles where the whole skull looks like it might make an exit out through the mouth at any moment. The kind of plastic smile you paste on your puss when your granny knits you an ugly sweater and you want her to know just how much you love it. There were tears in her eyes.

"I thought you knew," she said. It was then that I realized the random broken neck remark she'd made earlier in the car hadn't sat right with me. She knew an intimate detail; a detail only the killer would know. She also had the martial arts training to easily break a neck.

The gun in her hand wavered precariously like a deadly divining rod trying to choose a target on its own. It was obvious she hadn't called the ambulance and Rossi's posse was still miles away. Somebody was going to have to cool this situation down.

"Honey," I said gently, "why don't you put the gun down? Where's Liz?" I had a sickening feeling in my stomach. She had had a scuffle with Liz and Beau and over-powered them or worse. That would explain her bloody arm.

"You just don't get it, do you?" she asked, her voice beginning to break. "This is all just a game to you. Why couldn't you just have loved me? All of this could've been avoided."

"What the hell is going on?" Hayes asked. "What has this got to do with Vickie?"

Rosa addressed me with the answer.

"She was no good for you, either," she said. "You broke my heart."

The light bulb in my head began to flicker; I knew she was a little crazy about me, but she was also just plain crazy. The light bulb began to fizzle, then popped. She was killing off rivals for my affection.

"You killed them?" I shouted. "Because of me? Are you out of your mind?"

"We still have a chance," she said, tossing the envelope of photos on the edge of the bed. "We have the photos and he's loaded. We could get out of here and start a new life anywhere together."

Anyone could see there were too many bodies for this to work, not to mention the cabin's current audience. But desperation made it seem somewhat plausible to the judge. He shoved Hayes and took a last ditch lunge in my direction. I pointed the gun low at his legs and fired. Enough people had died already and corpses weren't gonna help clear my name. This time, for some reason, the bullet hit the intended target, striking Jenkins just above his right knee. He fell to the floor holding his leg. At this rate I was going to be able to actually hit something before the end of the night. I was getting the hang of this. I quit patting myself on the back when Mickey hollered.

"Frankie!" Mickey said. "Look out!" A shot rang out from behind me and a slug slammed into the wall inches from my head. One of the girls screamed. Mickey and Rosa were grappling for the gun and it went off two more times into the ceiling before Rosa turned, leaned into Mickey and flipped him over her shoulder and sent him flying into the wall. She pointed the gun at his face as he was pulling himself up. Mickey cringed. She pulled the trigger.

Click.

Again, click.

Misfire, empty magazine, good mojo; whatever you call it, the gun didn't go off. She cursed and threw it down and ran for the door.

Hayes seemed confused, pointing his gun wildly, not entirely sure who to hold it on. Everyone in the room was guilty of something.

"C'mon, man," I said. "There goes your killer." He stared at me blankly. "Hayes, let's go!"

I threw the old German hand cannon to Mickey and kept the late Lenny's .45 for myself.

"Keep an eye on his honor," I said as I ran out the door.

Chapter 42

Hayes and I ran out of the cabin and down the path toward the waterfalls. I could hear sirens approaching, finally. The unevenness of the path got the best of me and I took a spill, losing my gun in the process. It was just as well. I got up and limped my way toward the roar of the falls.

I called out to Rosa. I'm not sure why I went after her, but I did. My eyes took forever to adjust and I had to move slowly. The moon gave what little faint blue-ish assistance it could and I eventually saw her.

"Wait here," I told Hayes. "I think I can talk to her." His negotiating style wasn't cut out for this. I didn't have one at all, so I lied. "I know just what to say," I said.

I had no idea what I was going to say, but that hadn't stopped me before.

She was pacing back and forth, dangerously close to the edge of the falls. She was still humming that tune I couldn't make out. When she saw me her foot caught and she almost fell. I jumped towards her and she yelled.

"Don't," she said. "Don't come any closer."

Her crying had subsided some and she looked relatively placid and beautiful. What tears remained sparkled in the moonlight and for a brief instant I began to rationalize. I began to weigh my options. Sure, she was crazy, a prime candidate for the giggle factory, but hey, weren't they all?

You know, you can beat a man up, shoot at him, frame him for murder, generally make his life a living hell and yet plug a beautiful woman somewhere into the equation and all of a sudden it all doesn't seem so bad. This would one day be my undoing, no doubt, in fact, it already was.

Yeah, I could've fallen for Rosa and got in deep enough that I couldn't get out once the emotional instability and unbalance began to teeter and crack. I had been fortunate enough to pick up on it a little before. That's exactly why we were here, a trail of broken hearts and broken necks behind us. Perhaps this was the price for my accelerated bachelorhood. Blood was running down her arm from where Beau had bit her.

"Honey," I said, "let's get you some help. It's going to be okay." I reached for her and she moved away. She slipped a little and few rocks broke free and rattled over the edge. She started to laugh.

"Watch out," she said. "Or they'll say you killed me, too. It's all gonna be on you, Frankie. It'll be your word against the judge's. And Mickey's a lowlife; who'll believe him? Jenkins has got charisma, clout and cash. He'll walk and you'll hang."

Hayes was a few beats behind.

"What's she going on about?" he asked.

I motioned my hand down for him to stand by. This was a delicate situation. I could faintly hear a commotion coming from the direction of the cabin. I wasn't out of the woods yet. I kept at trying to defuse Rosa.

"What about you?" I asked her, stalling for time.

"What about me?" she repeated defiantly.

A bright light shone on us from the hill. Finally, the cavalry had arrived. Half a dozen or so New York State Troopers came barreling down toward us behind a constellation of bobbing flashlights, their guns drawn. But my heart dropped when I saw Jenkins limping up front, leading the charge. The silver tongued bastard had charmed them somehow. Mickey was charming, but not when it came to wooing cops. So naturally they made the obvious choice as to whose story actually held water and sided with Jenkins. I should have killed the bastard when I had the chance. Sure enough, Mickey brought up the rear escorted by two uniforms. He was in handcuffs.

"That's him," Jenkins said hoarsely. "Arrest that man." What do you know? Things were actually getting worse. Besides the five murders that I could very well look good for, there was another corpse on the scene. There was a potential witness I had shot. And now there was a judge—a judge I had shot—pointing the finger at me.

They all drew down on me and Hayes with an assortment of artillery. Hayes was still holding his gun; mine was in the bushes somewhere. The shouting began.

"Drop your weapon! Drop your weapon!" they shouted utterly out of unison like baying dogs. I instinctively put my hands up. Hayes reluctantly dropped his gun before joining me in my reach for the sky.

And like that they were upon me, throwing me to the ground and handcuffing me. The heavy knee in my back made it hard to breathe, but I knew better than to resist. I was going to have to keep cool if I wanted to be the least bit convincing. They hauled me up on my feet to come face to face with the judge. He wound up and punched me in the gut.

"You're gonna fry for this, Valentine," he said.

"Not when they see the photos," I said loudly for all to hear. Jenkins' trademark smile had returned, this time with a bit of dried blood in the corners. He pulled a quick over-the-shoulder glance, leaned close to my ear and spoke in a low voice.

"You mean these pictures here?" he asked, tapping

his breast pocket. "You and your crazy girlfriend here are going down for it all."

Hayes still seemed a little stunned, but was close enough to hear Jenkins. It was slowly coming into focus as he addressed the judge.

"You forgot," Hayes said. "One more witness: me."

Jenkins threw his head back and laughed.

"An ex-trigger happy cop who can't stand the fact that his kid was a whore? But don't get me wrong, she was a swell piece."

Hayes broke loose from the two troopers at his side and head-butted the judge. Jenkins' beak made a low, dull crunching sound as blood immediately spewed like a crimson lawn sprinkler. Two troopers grabbed him and pulled him away from Hayes.

"Let me go, let me go, goddammit," Jenkins said as he sputtered blood.

As the cops tried to contain the situation, Rosa made her move. Like a panther she grabbed Jenkins' hair from behind. His head wrenched back as she pulled him down, forcing him to his knees at her feet. Several troopers moved towards her, but backed off when they realized how close to the edge she was standing.

"Shoot her! Shoot her!" the judge screamed. "This bitch is crazy."

Rosa crouched down behind the judge, restraining him in an expert headlock.

"Shhh," she told him as he struggled. The more he squirmed, the more she tightened her hold and slowly began to choke him. With the falls behind her and the wall of law enforcement in front, there was nowhere for her to go. She looked up to address the troopers. She spoke calmly, so calmly it had the reverse effect. Everyone else was wound up like an eight-day clock. For the moment, nobody really seemed in charge. Rosa held all the cards...and the judge. She began slowly rocking back and forth. There were tears in her eyes, but she wasn't crying.

"I killed Vickie Hayes," she said. "Yeah, that's right. And I killed Gail Donovan, too. I guess I'm a little jealous. Blackmail was Vickie's idea. She didn't even want a payoff. She just wanted this jerk's attention and I know how that feels," she said with a pointed stare in my direction. "Mickey had nothing to do with exploiting the Honorable Preston Jenkins. I didn't either, that is until Donovan came sniffing around."

She spilled the whole thing candidly and even took a few liberties with the truth.

"Jenkins killed Donovan and the heavy up there on the hill," she said, stroking the judge's white hair as if he were a kitten. "You'll find the innkeeper tied up behind the counter in the lobby. The dog's locked in the powder room. He did that, too."

Jenkins sputtered and struggled.

"You lying bitch," he screamed.

She cuffed him across the mouth hard and reached into his jacket pocket. She pulled out the envelope of photos and tossed them at the feet of the trooper who appeared to be in charge.

With her hand still in Jenkins' hair she stood up and jerked the judge's head almost all the way around, breaking his neck with several loud pops. Before his body could completely slump to the ground, Rosa took a step backwards and winked at me as she and the judge disappeared over the edge. She didn't make a sound.

"No...!" got stuck in my throat as I ran to the edge of the falls. I fell to my knees and just stared silently over the edge of the falls into the blackness. I could just make out her pale frame, twisted unnaturally on the rocks below next to Jenkins.

I hadn't noticed Rossi standing next to me.

"Take these cuffs off him," he said. "Let him go."

Epilogue

It was a seriously salacious scandal to say the least, splashed all over the papers for the next week or so with its colorful cast of characters. You couldn't make this stuff up. It was like something right out of a movie—a transvestite judge, a dirty cop, a coupla private snoops, a bubbly call girl, nude models, jealous lovers, sad drunks, fathers bent on revenge, blackmail, a body count and some cat who liked to take pictures of pretty girls.

Rosa had hooked Jenkins up with Vickie as she did with a lot of high-end clients. Jenkins had a particular itch needing to be scratched. That's where Mickey came in. But Rosa would never have agreed to shaking down one of her high-end clients, unless that is, she got cut in for a taste. In setting the whole thing in motion, my name came up. Rosa confronted Vickie about me, things got out of hand, they fought and Vickie wound up dead.

Conway saw a shakedown as a shortcut to a bigger payoff rather than wasting shoe leather tracking down some dirty pictures for his crumby day rate. So Jenkins had Lenny see if the shamus could fly. Chapman wasn't involved, but the judge was cleaning up with broad strokes and the poor slob just got in the way.

Donovan had dealings with Rosa before and they had a pre-existing arrangement. She paid him protection and got him laid on a regular basis so she could run her business uninterrupted. Her snuffed-out pink smokes in the ashtray put her at the crime scene before Jenkins ever put Donovan wise to the photos. Donovan knew that her being there weighed in somehow, he just wasn't sure exactly how. So once Jenkins had Conway eliminated for essentially the same thing that ultimately got Donovan's ticket punched, Jenkins sent him to find the photos. Donovan just figured Rosa and Vickie were running a badger game on Jenkins.

When no photos turned up at Vickie's, Donovan roughed up Rosa in his search. He probably beat my name out of her even though it was already on his short list. When he did finally find the photos in my car, instead of handing them over to the judge, he thought he was smart, tried to parlay it all into a juicy payday and wound up being taken off the payroll permanently.

Oh, and of course there was my old pal Mickey. He was a real stand up guy, handling himself admirably at the showdown at the Chalet, sustaining a gunshot wound and backing up my story all the way despite the fact I was the one who shot him. He got a tattoo over the wound. So now his shoulder has a heart with a real bullet hole in it. The girls seemed to love it, especially the two models with him that night at the Chalet.

"They're gonna wear me out, Frankie," he said over coffee at the diner one morning a few weeks later. His eyelids were at half mast. His clothes were a wreck and it looked like he had combed his hair with a brick. Mickey wasn't getting much sleep. It seems he couldn't make up his mind between the two girls, so he was dating both.

Me? One seemed like one too many for the time being.

"Yeah, well, I'm gonna take a little break from the girlies," I said.

We both sat looking at each other before busting out into laughter—a couple of bachelor buffoons.

"You're tellin' me you're gonna take a break from life, liberty and the happiness of pursuit?" Mickey said between snorts. "C'mon."

"I am," I said. "Really. For at least a coupla days."

I meant it. I wanted to mean it anyway. But I knew myself better than that. I couldn't stay away from those sweet fine things even if I wanted to. They were in my blood and under my skin. And let's face it, if the events surrounding Vickie's death hadn't dampened my desire, well then, nothing would. Still, a break from all the static might be nice. I wasn't going to avoid them altogether and join the Jesuits; I just wouldn't be on the prowl. Yeah, just a little breather...an intermission, if you will.

Mickey was on to bigger and better things himself. He was off to Hollywood to meet with investors and audition some new prospects for a feature length film. Stag reels confined his budding creativity and so did this little upstate burgh.

And Mickey was a visionary.

"Just picture it, Frankie," he said, outlining an invisible marquee in the air with his hand. "The real Sodom and Gomorrah, but with all that juicy stuff the Bible danced around. Plenty of smut, but substance as well—actual plots, sets other than motel rooms and fly-by-night warehouses and honest to goodness acting."

Uh-huh, a real visionary.

I wished him luck and we agreed to get together when he came back. He wished me luck on my romantic hiatus.

"A sawbuck says it doesn't last through the end of the day," he said out his car window.

"You're on, sucker," I said with a wave. I stood and watched until his car disappeared around the corner.

For the first time in a while, I felt good. Nothing was hanging over my head. It was a gorgeous late September morning with just a hint of autumn in the air. I turned and strolled back towards the diner with a renewed cut in my strut and glide in my stride. I shielded my eyes from the sun just in time to see her.

A young lady by the car parked next to mine was wrestling with coffee in a to-go cup and a bag of donuts as she rummaged around in her purse for her keys. Her yellow dress was sexy and just the right amount of tight as if she'd been poured into it and forgot to say when. She seemed to have the situation under control, but that fine frame perched on open toe high heels warranted a closer look. And perhaps, the aid of a gentleman.

"Need a hand?" I asked.

"Thanks, I got it," she said, keeping the coffee cup level with her chin. She looked up just long enough that her purse shifted forward, the donuts hit the ground and hot coffee spilled down the front of her dress. She let out a little yell. In an instant I was dabbing at the coffee, perhaps a little too enthusiastically, with my handkerchief.

"I think you got it all," she said, annoyed while pulling my hands from her chest. She pulled down her sunglasses and glared at me.

"Oh, I'm sorry," I said. "I just didn't want you to get burned."

I smiled sheepishly and after a moment she smiled back.

"C'mon," I said, "lemme buy you a fresh one."

"You're a fresh one," she said with a hint of a glint of flirt in her eyes. And wow, was she a gorgeous one.

I kicked off the how-do-you-do's.

"My name's Frankie Valentine," I said.

Her eyebrows went up.

"Valentine?" she asked. "Really? And what do you do, Mister Valentine?"

"I take pictures of pretty girls," I said.

She rolled her eyes as if she'd heard it all before.

I persisted and finally convinced her I owed her a coffee.

"At least for the pat-down anyway," I said. We walked back into the diner. And with any luck I was going to owe Mickey ten bucks.

Grift'n'Grind

A Frankie Valentine Short Story

Grift'n'Grind

A Frankie Valentine Short Story

I was chasing a few ice cubes at the bottom of my bourbon and soda when she brushed passed me in a flash of satin, chiffon and Chanel. Lilliana looked back and winked. But it wasn't a flirtatious salutation, it was my cue. I sat up straight. The bum across the room in her crosshairs was ripe and ready. The loud lout had lushed, gushed and ga-ga'd over the gals long enough. Sure, that's what they were there for, but this jackass had no class.

Playing "he loves me, he loves me not" with the fingers of her long black opera gloves, she crossed The Palace floor.

The Palace fancied itself a class joint and at a glance didn't look all that bad. The velvet was worn around the edges and the wood a little scuffed up, but with the dim light, all its scars and history faded into the shadows. Yet in the security of this dark obscurity, it was nothing more than a dead end grind house percolating with punks, pariahs, pinheads, panty sniffers and pigs.

They squealed and grunted for The Palace pretties. The Palace had a rather impressive stable of fine fillies despite the desperate degenerates it drew. Just like this low life.

He was what the gals called an international customer: Russian hands and Roman fingers.

In his custom-tailored silver sharkskin suit and his moist mitts full of green, he acted as if he could buy his way into or out of anything. He threw money like confetti. He blew smoke. He spilled as much as he drank. His two cronies were equally obnoxious as they egged him on. He leered. He was lewd, rude and crude. And the way he pawed the cocktail waitresses... well, they'd had enough. He had it coming. I could see the pieces slowly fall into place from my perch at the end of the bar. I got my camera ready.

Me? I'm Frankie Valentine and I take pictures.

I had shot enough crime scenes for my day gig as a crime scene photographer with the city police department that I could practically see when a new one was in the works.

So I spent my daytime clicking shots of dead things outlined in chalk and nighttime and I spent my nighttime doing candid vanity shots of the local glitterati for two bucks a pop as they wined and dined on top of the line grub at Sweeney's Supper Club.

Sweeney's was swank.

Everything from the maitre d's smile to the silverware sparkled. Even the carpet had some cosmic luster as if you were walking on the nighttime sky. They had a first rate band and put on quite a floor show Thursday through Sunday. If you happened to be one of this town's society swells, it was common knowledge that you hadn't officially arrived until you were part of the Sweeney's scene. And a picture would prove you were there.

I'd capture first dates, anniversaries, birthdays or folks just having a night out on the town. If I happened to photograph, say, a City Councilman whose date was definitely not Mrs. City Councilman, I'd really add to my greenback stack. Boy, those civil servants could be quite generous; not only by taking their "niece" out to a nice dinner, but by paying a lot more than I typically charged for their picture. Why, some had even offered to buy the negatives from me. But I don't want them to think I'm there to put the squeeze on them...I'm just taking pictures of everyone down at Sweeney's.

Sweeney's and The Palace backed up to one another. It was a quick trip from one back door to the next. The shared alley at the rear of both establishments was filthy and narrow, much like the line separating each one's clientele. I saw no difference between the con artist or pervert bellied up at The Palace bar or the banker making handshake deals while choking down filet mignon at Sweeney's. The eagle flies one way or another. It really just depends on how you make your money, what you are willing to do for it.

When I wasn't drawing a paycheck with the police or shaking down blue bloods for a deuce at a time, I shot glamour girls, pin-ups and nudie cuties. I had regular girlie photo spreads in magazines like *Cavalier*, *Modern Man* and *Swank*. The kind of breed I sought to pose for these pictures, worked at or frequented The Palace; so naturally, I did too.

Whenever I had a break at Sweeney's, I'd pop through the alley, avoiding rats the size of motorcycles as they raided the garbage, making careful not to trip over anyone laying there, and into my own little sin-riddled Shangri-la.

Every night was a gas even when jokers like this forgot their manners at the door. But he was gonnna get his. Like I said, I could see it all fall into place. So could Ronnie.

Ronnie Watt and Them That Play It Hot was the name of the band that shook The Palace's foundation while the gals shook everything else. They were all top-flight players; many of them had even played in the big band at Sweeney's at one time or another, but demotions from things like dope, dames and dice had them traveling through the alley to The Palace where things like dope, dames and dice didn't matter.

They were working a casual vamp that swung low and slow like an elephant trunk, when Ronnie suddenly raised his hand for them to shift gears.

"Wake up, boys," Ronnie said. "It's show time. *Harlem Nocturne*, reeeeal slow. Lil's stalking her prey."

Ronnie counted off three narcotic snaps so far apart they were in three different postal codes. The bass player and drummer kicked in so slow they were almost playing backwards. Ronnie leaned into his sax snaky and sly; the same way Lilliana approached her mark.

Lilliana was a dark brown Latin lovely from Bogota, Columbia, with long black hair, even longer legs and a front end that stood out like a balcony. And boy, could she move. She knew how to grind a sucker into dust—or mud if you considered his sweat. Gyrating an inch from his face she would tease him within an inch of his life. In her husky purr, she would tell him it was *La Danza del Amor*.

The dance of love.

Better known around here as the grift'n'grind. It was simple; he'd pitch a tent, she'd pick his pocket.

The ol' grift'n'grind.

You see, Ronnie Watt and Them That Play It Hot supplied the grooves for Lilliana's smooth moves. We had all seen this play out more than a few times. I had pictures to prove it.

The Palace manager, Monte, turned a blind eye to Lilliana's hustle on account she was a major draw. Other girls used their curves to work angles, but they had to cut Monte in.

Monte was low man on the syndicate's totem pole and an all around shifty shylock who ran numbers, peddled dope, extorted, exploited, enforced and pimped out the girls when their habits exceeded their tips. He was righteous trash, a serious scumbag. He was guilty of everything.

He was gaunt and pale with a third degree moon tan. His face was more terrain than complexion. He splashed on too much aftershave and smelled like a barbershop in a landfill. His grin was as greasy as his thinning hair. He was constantly slicking it back.

Lilliana phoned in her routine most of the time. The poor slobs and stage door Johnnies that usually crowded ringside by the runway just didn't rate. Most were smart enough not to look for love on the avenue; nobody wants to wind up doing the penicillin polka, after all. But they were still hapless and horny and if it weren't for these sub rosa sojourns to The Palace for a look-see to re-stock the spank bank, they would be forced to survive on what got dished out with a grudge on anniversaries and Christmas.

When Lilliana did pull out her A-game, she gave it the berries. It seemed almost out of spite or revenge, with the lucky lap typically belonging to the loudest, rudest, asshole in the room. She'd get done with him and you'd have to set the guy on fire just to cool him down.

So, here we went again.

Her torso was twisting in low gear as she made her way to his table. With his bloodshot glims glommed onto her fine frame, he snuffed his cigar out on the table next to the ashtray. He smoothed his hair. He licked his lips. I could hear him swallow. He put his arms out to his sides pushing his two pals behind him. Lilliana continued closer. She swayed hypnotic. Her mark grinned demonic.

"Mine," he said. "All mine."

The gloves were off by the time she reached him.

Ronnie and the boys rounded the turn into the bridge.

Lilliana's hips locked into the drums and her spine walked the bass line. She slithered and slinked. Nobody blinked.

Within moments she had his jacket around his shoulders, one side of his collar was up and his pants were several inches shorter...and counting. He tried to stand up and she pushed him back into his seat, tossing her head back and laughing. His mug was fire engine red. Lilliana was wearing his tie, sliding it around her neck and between her breasts. She straddled him, hovering over his lap while redirecting his hands. A few of the other dancers were on the stage hashing out their routines, but all eyes were fixed on *La Danza del Amor.* The crowd began to whoop and cheer.

The weight of the camera around my neck reminded me to get some pictures of the rapidly accelerating goings-on. I had had the occasion to shoot Lilliana's portrait before and she and I made a little cash on the side with guys like this who—upon sobering up—were so overcome with guilt and remorse and a sore back from sleeping on a park bench, that they'd buy back the photos in order to keep the home fires safely lit. It was the least they could do. It would be our little secret.

So, I peered through the viewfinder and started banging away while Lilliana touched, teased, taunted, tickled, tugged and tantalized. It was getting good, real good. She brought her lips towards his and breathed hot. She slipped her hand inside his jacket.

Out of nowhere Monte stepped in. He snagged Lilliana's arm. A chorus of discontent filled the room with boos and hisses. Monte was unfazed.

"Try that crap in here again and you're history toots!" he said a little too loud. Lilliana twisted her arm free and stormed off.

"Bastard," she said to Monte.

Monte looked over at the would-be mark.

"Sorry, Mister Grasso," he said. "These broads, heh-heh, you gotta keep your eye on 'em."

We had never heard of him or seen him before. Another one of Monte's mob chums we figured. Based on all of Monte's cow-towing, he was probably higher up on the food chain than Monte.

Mister Grasso was oblivious to his impending donation and seemed more concerned with *La Danza del Amor's* early curtain. He was getting hot and started to stand up.

"Look, you," he said." You'd better..."

Not missing a beat, Monte cut him off with a snap of his fingers. Two beauties appeared out of nowhere and got to work. They sat him back down and made with the confection and affection. But bless their hearts; they were bush league compared to what had previously kept his lap warm.

"Beat it, you!" he said dismissing the two girls with a wave of his arm. In doing so he caught one of the girls in the mouth with the back of his hand. She gasped and put her hand to her mouth. She saw blood and then she saw red. With a shriek, she was on him clawing at his face like a rabid cat. Tables began to empty quick-like as folks made their way to the exit. Grasso stood up, shoved her back and slapped her hard. She probably shouldn't have come back at him but she did; these Palace gals were tough. He hit her again, this time with his closed fist. It made a dull cracking sound and she fell to the floor in a heap. She didn't move; neither did Monte. He just stood there worthless and stunned.

Any other joker would have been roughed up and tossed out at this point, so we figured clearly this guy had some juice. That would've explained Monte's momentary paralysis. His beady eyes darted back and forth between the girl on the floor and Grasso, his fist balled up, his eyes full of rage. You could cut the tension with a chainsaw.

The Palace guards, Tiny, Tony and Teddy—the Three

T's as they were known—were there to enforce the "no touching" policy and to roust the rowdies. They were rarely, if ever, challenged, their brawn served as a kind of diplomatic deterrent...usually.

Tiny was a soft-spoken six-foot tall, five-foot wide Italian kid who cordially attempted to reseat Mister Grasso only to be thanked with a sucker punch. One of Grasso's chums slugged Tony who in turn picked him up and threw him over the bar crashing into a phalanx of liquor bottles. Teddy joined Tiny in trying to pin Grasso and all three crashed into a row of tables whose occupants joined in by exchanging blows with each other. Within seconds, the whole damn room exploded. Chairs and bottles were airborne. The sound of broken glass, and shouts and screams threatened to drown out *Harlem Nocturne*. I had squeezed off a couple of shots of Lilliana's dance, but didn't want my camera or my head busted, so I got behind the bar, poured myself a bourbon and ducked down for the duration.

The Palace always had a short fuse. With a lot of the clientele, just one drink or one wink away from throwing a punch. It always amazed me how just one fight could spark a multitude of little unrelated fights which were brewing all night throughout a room. It always amazed me even more, that as the fists were swinging so was the band.

This was a particularly heated bruhaha and a good deal of the brawlers wound up getting hauled off in the paddy wagon, including this Grasso character. By the time the dust had settled, the place looked like a tornado had blown through it.

Another night at The Palace.

Typically, we would have a good laugh at closing time, Lilliana would slide the band a taste for their part in the grift'n'grind, they'd blow it at the bar and that would be it. By the time whatever rube she had rolled sobered up, the whole scene would be a blur.

But Monte had lowered the boom before Lilliana could let her fingers do the walking, so tonight it was ixnay on the payday.

Or so we thought.

By the time I made it to the little dressing room, Lilliana was sitting at her dressing table half undressed. I had photographed her here before.

The little room was set up for the girls, but musicians who didn't stare and photographers with a vested artistic interest could hang out in this shabby sanctuary littered with G-strings and pretty things made of sequins and feathers and little else. The checkerboard floor had never seen a mop, the walls were smoke stained a dull yellow and the lock on the door didn't work. There were bars on the windows overlooking the alley. There were blown out lights running along the mirrors lining the walls over the counter. The working ones cast weird shadows on the girl's faces. I imagined that's how they saw themselves; dark, mysterious, incomplete as their reflections stared back along with a taped up picture here or there of a boyfriend or a child being raised by his babysitter while mom brought home the bacon one strip at a time.

But Lilliana wasn't looking in the mirror. She was staring down at a wallet; *the* wallet. It looked well fed, just like its former owner.

I looked at the wallet.

I looked at Lilliana.

I looked at the wallet again.

There was a lot of green peeking out...a lot, all C-notes. I started to laugh. Boy, she was quick. Despite the melee, Lilliana had kept her eyes on the prize and landed a big one.

"Honey, you really know how to...I mean you are real...what's the matter?" I said.

She just sat there dazed.

"Okay, baby," I said, "I'll bite, what gives?"

"Count it," she said, a smile slowly beginning to crack.

I counted. I counted high.

"Jesus Christ," I said. "There's over ten thousand dollars here."

You've gotta understand, for a lot of these goons it wasn't worth the hassle to chase after a beat-up billfold with a couple of fins, a dried up jimmy hat and faded snaps of the kiddies. But ten large? You could bet someone was going to be coming back for this. And I, for one, didn't want to be around when he did.

"Honey, you gotta give this back," I said. "If Monte gets wise to this we're all through...or worse. That character's obviously connected."

She stood up so quick she up-ended her chair; it fell to the floor with a bang. She pulled my tie, tugging me towards her. She breathed hot in my face.

"Keep it between us and I'll split it with you," she said. "That jerk won't be out of jail until Monday."

I pushed my hat back and scratched my head. On one hand, it was a nice chunk of change. On the other, if I got mixed up in this I might wind up getting mixed up in concrete.

As I considered my options, Ronnie and the boys bounced in. They were still fired up from the fight.

"Boy, Monte sure is a jerk," one of them said.

"Yeah, Lil," said the other, "you practically had that cad in the bag until ol' killjoy killed joy."

Before they could see it, I quickly stuffed the wallet in my jacket pocket and joined in on the Monte bashing.

"Yeah," I said, trying to conjure up some of that old altar boy sincerity. "Nuts to him. Don't you worry, Lil, there'll be more. This place is lousy with 'em. Hell, you oughta know that by now."

It was an Oscar-winning performance. She acted real steamed, cursing Monte and men in general under and over her breath, throwing her things in her little blue suitcase, stomping around loudly. We all took a step back. I wondered if she had ever been an altar boy.

I offered to walk her home. This elicited jabs and whispers from everyone in the room.

Two more dancers had come in and were changing into their street clothes. They were half dressed and full of whispers and giggles, looking at me.

"I don't know," I overheard one say to the other. "I think he's cute."

"I'm walking her home," I said "And that's it."

That and divvying up my ticket out of here. Five grand would get me out of here and set up nice in Hollywood.

It was a quick ten minute stroll to her three-story walk up. *Naturally, I'll have to go up to split the green*, I thought to myself. *Maybe have a cup of coffee, go back to my pad, pack a grip and make tracks.*

We sat in her little kitchen, split a root beer and the loot. We had a few laughs at Monte's expense and discussed plans like strangers do when you know you will never see that person again.

I told her about Hollywood and suggested she give it a go as well. She smiled and looked far off. She said something about going home.

It's the most we had ever talked. All those nights watching her dance, watching her hustle, it wasn't until now that I realized how intoxicatingly seductive her charms could be. Just the way she walked from the table to the icebox was an event.

A gentleman can be gentle for just so long before gentle takes a walk leaving the man standing alone to resist or not. I learned somewhere a long time ago, it's only temptation when you resist.

Who knows? Maybe she really thought I was as handsome as she led me to believe. She was slick, boy. She played me like a cheap violin at a saps convention. She hung on every word I said, laughed at every joke. I was a sensation.

When she sat on my lap, I managed to play it cool. Same thing when she mussed my hair. It's when she planted a juicy kiss on my mouth with those juicy lips that I knew I was in trouble. She kissed me again, harder, longer.

That's about all I remember.

Kissing was not in the cards. Spending the night was not in the cards. Having my way with a girl as fine as Lilliana wasn't in the cards

Apparently neither was five grand.

When I awoke in her bed the next morning, I was feeling pretty good. We had made love. We had ten grand between us. We were getting the hell outta here.

I rolled over for a glimpse and a kiss. *We* weren't there. I called out to her.

Nothing.

I got up to look around.

Nothing.

The sun blasted through the bedroom window to illuminate the dust in the air. That's all there was. The closet door was open with nothing but the empty dangle of a few lonely hangers. She was gone. The money was gone.

I sat down on the edge of the bed and started to laugh. Yup, the old grift'n'grind. There was a note on the bedside table that caught my eye. I read it and started to laugh.

"I'll think of you whenever they play *Harlem Nocturne*", it said.

ACKNOWLEDGEMENTS

Thanks to my literary sensei, Charles Benoit for all his guidance, Jason Smith for the killer cover, Lou Boxer at Noircon for the enthusiasm and the connections, my Mom (Susan De Blase), Dayna Papaleo, Elissa Orlando, Emily and Jürgen Miller and Liz Waller for the early look-see, Dusty Fox for the final copy edits, and the fine folks at Down & Out Books for the thumbs-up.

ABOUT THE AUTHOR

Frank De Blase is an award-winning writer, photographer, ex-rockabilly crooner, social contrarian, and all-around troublemaker who always leaves room for desert.

His writing and photography has been published in LEG SHOW, LEG WORLD, SWANK, ULTRA, TEMPTRESS, RETRO LOVELY TABOO, OL' SKOOL RODZ, CAR KULTURE DELUXE, REBEL INK, SKIN AND INK, URBAN INK, V MAGAZINE, DOWNBEAT, and CITY NEWSPAPER.

De Blase lives in Rochester, New York, with his wife, Deborah. This is his first novel for Down & Out Books.

http://www.frankdeblase.com/

OTHER TITLES FROM DOWN AND OUT BOOKS

See www.DownAndOutBooks.com for complete list

By J.L. Abramo
Catching Water in a Net
Clutching at Straws
Counting to Infinity
Gravesend
Chasing Charlie Chan (*)

By Trey R. Barker
2,000 Miles to Open Road
Road Gig: A Novella
Exit Blood

By Richard Barre
The Innocents
Bearing Secrets
Christmas Stories
The Ghosts of Morning
Blackheart Highway
Burning Moon
Echo Bay (*)
Lost (*)

By Milton T. Burton
Texas Noir

By Reed Farrel Coleman
The Brooklyn Rules

By Tom Crowley
Vipers Tail (*)

By Jack Getze
Big Numbers (*)
Big Money (*)
Big Mojo (*)

By Keith Gilman
Bad Habits (*)

By Jon & Ruth Jordan
Murder and Mayhem in Muskego (Editors)

By Bill Moody
Czechmate
The Man in Red Square

By Gary Phillips
The Perpetrators
Scoundrels (Editor)

By Lono Waiwaiole
Wiley's Lament
Wiley's Shuffle
Wiley's Refrain
Dark Paradise

(*)—Coming Soon

CPSIA information can be obtained at www.ICGtesting.com
Printed in the USA
LVOW07s0321130415

434323LV00001B/5/P